Lizzie & Lucky

The Mystery of the Lost Chicken

Megan Rix

Illustrated by Tim Budgen

PUFFIN

PUFFIN BOOKS

UK | USA | Canada | Ireland | Australia
India | New Zealand | South Africa

Puffin is part of the Penguin Random House group of companies
whose addresses can be found at global.penguinrandomhouse.com.

www.penguin.co.uk
www.puffin.co.uk
www.ladybird.co.uk

Penguin Random House UK

First published by Puffin Books 2023

001

Set in Bembo MT Std
Text design by Janene Spencer
Printed in Great Britain by Clays Ltd, Elcograf S.p.A.

The authorized representative in the EEA is Penguin Random House Ireland,
Morrison Chambers, 32 Nassau Street, Dublin D02YH68

A CIP catalogue record for this book is available from the British Library

ISBN: 978–0–241–59605–0

All correspondence to:
Puffin Books
Penguin Random House Children's, One Embassy Gardens
8 Viaduct Gardens, London SW11 7BW

PUFFIN BOOKS

Lizzie & Lucky

The Mystery of the Lost Chicken

Megan Rix is the hugely popular author of animal adventure books set in the modern day and key periods of history. An animal advocate and dog-friend, Megan draws inspiration from her own adorable dogs Traffy, Bella, Freya and Ellie.

Follow Megan Rix on Twitter
@megan_rix
#LizzieandLucky

Books by Megan Rix

THE GREAT FIRE DOGS
THE BOMBER DOG
THE GREAT ESCAPE
THE VICTORY DOGS
A SOLDIER'S FRIEND
THE RUNAWAYS
ECHO COME HOME
THE HERO PUP
THE PAW HOUSE
THE LOST WAR DOG

For younger readers

ROSA AND THE DARING DOG
WINSTON AND THE MARMALADE CAT
EMMELINE AND THE PLUCKY PUP
FLORENCE AND THE MISCHIEVOUS KITTEN

Lizzie and Lucky:

THE MYSTERY OF THE MISSING PUPPIES
THE MYSTERY OF THE STOLEN TREASURE
THE MYSTERY OF THE DISAPPEARING RABBIT

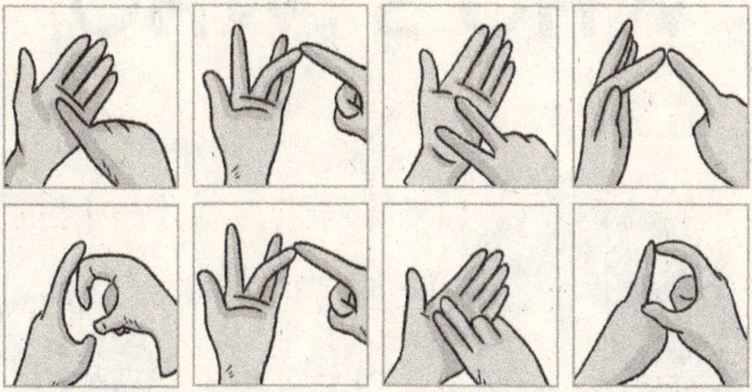

Be kind to every kind x

– M.R.

To Julia, thank you x

– T.B.

WHO'S WHO

Lizzie

Lucky

Ted

Carla

Dad
Mum
Auntie Rita

CHAPTER 1

It was late morning on the first day of the summer holidays. Eight-year-old detective Lizzie and her Dalmatian puppy, Lucky, were playing hide-and-seek with their best friend, Ted.

Ted was looking for a good place to hide while Lizzie and Lucky waited in Lizzie's bedroom.

'. . . Ninety-eight, ninety-nine, one hundred. . .' Lizzie counted in sign language before adding, 'Coming, ready or not!'

Lucky looked up at Lizzie and wagged her tail. She loved to play hide-and-seek. Dogs' noses can smell far better than a human's can, and Lucky's ears were very sensitive to sound too. That made her very good at finding people.

Lizzie made the sign for **'find'**.

Lucky knew exactly what she had to do, and headed straight out of Lizzie's bedroom door.

While Lucky used her nose to sniff out Ted's scent downstairs, Lizzie looked for signs of Ted upstairs: a door left slightly ajar, a rug corner turned over. There were always clues to be found.

But Ted wasn't there.

Lizzie headed downstairs and into the lounge. Her mum and dad were curled up on the sofa together. Mum's hair was bright pink, and her hearing aids were adorned with tiny stars. She loved art and had decorated both Lizzie and Lizzie's dad's hearing aids too. Even Lucky's collar was extra sparkly now.

Mum and Dad were watching the regional news on TV.

'Where's the interpreter?' signed Dad.

Lizzie could see he was cross.

'It's not right,' signed Mum.

There were only a few times during the day when the news was translated into sign language.

Lizzie checked behind the curtains and under the sofa Mum and Dad were sitting on, but Ted wasn't hiding there either. *Where could he be?*

Dad was about to turn the TV off when Lizzie saw her mum suddenly grab his arm. She pointed at the screen, and Dad's mouth opened wide in shock.

Lizzie looked at the TV too. It was

showing footage from Kenton, the town closest to where Mum's sister, Rita, lived. Auntie Rita ran her animal sanctuary there called the Five Freedoms.

But she wasn't at the sanctuary now.

Auntie Rita was on the TV – **in handcuffs**!

Before they could understand what was happening, the news ended and the screen changed to the weather forecast. The news might not think Auntie Rita being arrested was important enough to focus on for long, but Lizzie did.

Lucky came running into the lounge with Lizzie's mum's phone in her mouth. Its *message received* light was flashing.

One of the things Lizzie and Lucky practised a lot was alerting. Sometimes Lizzie didn't notice the flashing message alert light on her phone. But Lucky always heard everyone's phones, and she knew phone alerting was a very, very important job – just like doorbell and oven-timer alerting.

Lizzie took the phone from Lucky and made the sign for **'thank you'**, before giving the puppy a stroke and handing the phone over to her mum.

'Why's my sister been arrested?' Mum signed, shaking her head in disbelief. The footage had been so brief before it had moved on.

Dad flicked through the other TV channels, but their local news wasn't showing on any of them.

'We have to help her,' signed Lizzie's dad, and Lizzie nodded. The mystery of why Auntie Rita had been arrested must be solved.

Ted came into the lounge from his hiding place in the garden. He'd thought the prickly bush had been a good place to hide – although a bit uncomfortable – but he hadn't expected Lizzie and Lucky to take this long to find him.

'What's happened?' he signed. Ted wasn't deaf like Lizzie and her parents, but he was very good at signing. He immediately knew something was very wrong from looking at everyone's faces.

'Auntie Rita's been arrested,' Lizzie signed back. 'But we don't know why.'

The message light on the mobile phone flashed again.

'It says, "**Help.** Come ASAP!"' Mum signed. The message was from Auntie Rita, and Lizzie knew ASAP

meant 'as soon as possible'.

'Right,' signed Dad, jumping up. 'Let's get to Kenton police station. I'll drive.'

'I'm coming too,' signed Ted. 'I'll just let my gran know.'

Ted lived over the road with his gran, two rabbits, two rats and a grumpy cat called Ruby.

Lizzie's dad signed to him to be quick, and Ted dashed off.

Lizzie raced upstairs to grab her detective bag. It had inside it: a pair of small binoculars, a phone, a magnifying glass, a white-and-black light torch, a fingerprint kit, a wildlife crime information leaflet, clue bags, Mum's old tweezers, a pack of tissues, detective gloves, Lucky's dog whistle and ball, plus a notebook and pencil.

The detectives in the mystery stories she

loved to read often helped people who'd been wrongly arrested, and she was going to help her Auntie Rita.

Lizzie headed out of the house with her detective bag, and Lucky came after her, holding her octopus toy in her mouth. She'd had the toy ever since she'd come to live with Lizzie, and took it everywhere they went.

Dad was already in the car and Ted came running up as Lizzie clipped Lucky's harness on. Mum locked the front door and then got into the passenger seat, and Lizzie, Lucky and Ted climbed into the back.

As soon as everyone's seatbelts were secured, Lizzie made the sign for 'ready',

Dad started the engine and they zoomed off.

CHAPTER 2

Lucky was sitting on Lizzie's lap and looking out of the window as they drove into Kenton town centre.

There were lots of people blocking the roads and holding signs with writing on them. Some of the people were deaf and signing to each other, others were talking.

Out of the window Lizzie spotted Carla, who worked at Auntie Rita's animal sanctuary. Carla had a cochlear implant to help her hear and used a mixture of signing and speech. She was driving on the pavement in her high-tech yellow electric powerchair. It had been made especially for her, and Carla called it Lightning because the chair could go so fast.

Suddenly Carla swerved into the road right in front of their car. It was fortunate that they'd been driving slowly because of all the people protesting in the street. Lizzie's dad quickly pressed the brake pedal so that they didn't bump into Carla.

Dad sounded the horn, but Carla didn't stop. She only looked round and shook her fist at him, an angry expression on her face.

Lizzie could see Carla's mouth moving,

but she couldn't lip-read what she was saying because Carla was shouting.

'What did she say?' Lizzie signed to Ted.

Ted frowned and shook his head. 'I'm not sure, but it sounded like "*Don't hurt Lightning*."'

'That's the name of her powerchair,' Lizzie signed to him.

Carla whizzed over the road, narrowly missing a few of the protestors, and Lizzie saw where she was heading.

She tapped Dad urgently on the shoulder and pointed. The police station was just a little bit ahead of them.

Dad stopped the car as close to the station as he could. Other cars and lorries honked at Lizzie's dad for parking in the middle of the street. He couldn't stay there.

Mum, Lizzie, Lucky and Ted scrambled out.

'Join you in a minute,' Dad signed to them, and he drove on, looking for somewhere to park.

Last school term, Lizzie's class had done a project on the law and had visited their local police station. A police officer had talked to them about her job and taken their fingerprints, before showing them a pair of handcuffs – and the inside of a holding cell.

Lizzie had asked the police officer what her favourite part of the job was.

'I love protecting our precious wildlife,' the police officer had told her with a smile. Then she'd given Lizzie a leaflet about wildlife crime and the importance of preserving endangered species.

Lizzie had made the sign for 'thank you' and put the leaflet in her detective bag. The day had been very exciting.

But now Lizzie was feeling worried about Auntie Rita. How could she communicate if she was in handcuffs? It was different for hearing people – they could still talk if they had handcuffs on, but a person who used sign language couldn't.

Going into the police station, she also wondered if there would be anyone there who knew sign language. At least there was the 999 BSL app nowadays, as well as online interpreters. *Much better than it used to be in the old days*, as her mum and dad were always saying.

Inside the police station there were lots of people milling round the small reception area. Lizzie's mum squeezed her hand comfortingly.

Carla was there too.

CELLS
ENQUIRY DESK
ANIMAL RESCUE

'Your mobility scooter goes really fast,' Ted said to Carla.

Carla pulled a face. 'Lightning's not a mobility scooter – he's a powerchair. And not just any old powerchair,' she told him. 'Lightning's one of a kind and can go up to thirty miles an hour. He even has a tracking device and a secret compartment.'

She pressed a button and the bottom section under the seat, which was made of tinted glass, slid open.

Just then, Lizzie saw Auntie Rita come out of a side room. Her eyes were all red as if she'd been crying.

There was a lady with her, and Lizzie was very surprised to see Auntie Rita and the lady signing together. The police had called in a real-life interpreter – no need for a virtual one today. A police officer walked over to the pair and the interpreter nodded and went with her.

Lizzie's mum ran over and threw her arms round her sister. Lizzie, Lucky and Ted followed her.

'I had to join the protest,' Auntie Rita signed when she had given Mum a huge hug. 'The farmer next door to the sanctuary is going to sell his land to a company called Butterbrooks, and they're going to turn it into a chicken megafarm!'

'What's a megafarm?' Ted signed.

'It's a giant farm that keeps lots of animals in huge barns. They never even get to go outside,' Auntie Rita signed.

'How big are the barns?' Ted signed.

'Some of them can be as long as a football pitch,' Auntie Rita told him, and Ted looked shocked.

Lizzie was shocked too. A football pitch was over a hundred metres long. She tried to imagine one filled with lots and lots of chickens all squashed together.

Carla glided over to them.

'Someone should lock Mr Baron inside one of Butterbrooks's windowless barns. See how he likes it,' she said, and Lizzie lipread her.

Lizzie realized the neighbour's name must be Mr Baron.

'Butterbrooks just ignored us when we contacted them,' Auntie Rita signed.

But why was Mr Baron selling his farmland in the first place? Lizzie wondered.

'If you could meet with Mr Baron, maybe you could explain why it's a bad idea?' she signed.

Auntie Rita shook her head. 'We've sent letters and emails and tried and tried to see him, but all with no luck.'

'Five thousand people signed our petition,' Carla told them. 'But it wasn't enough to stop Mr Baron, so we had to do something more.'

'That's why we were protesting,' Auntie Rita signed to Lizzie, Mum and Ted. 'Only I didn't know I could be arrested for it. I was so frightened when they put the handcuffs on me, and worried about my animals at the sanctuary.'

Lizzie nodded. Now she understood why there'd been a protest, and the mystery of why Auntie Rita was arrested was solved – the megafarm sounded terrible. Lizzie wanted to find a way to stop Mr Baron from selling his land that didn't involve Auntie Rita – or any of them – getting in more trouble. She was glad she'd brought her detective bag along.

'Once Mr Baron has done the deal, it'll be too late. Butterbrooks could have their barns up in no time,' Auntie Rita finished. 'Just the thought of it makes me want to cry.'

She hugged Lizzie tight and kissed the top of her head. Lucky stood up on her back paws and snuggled in too, not wanting to be left out, and Mum wrapped her arms around them all.

'It's OK now,' Mum signed, rubbing her sister's back.

Ted and Carla exchanged a look. *Was it really going to be OK?*

At that moment the interpreter came back, and signed that the paperwork was all done and Rita was free to go.

Auntie Rita thanked her for all her help and then turned to Lizzie and Ted.

'Let's go home,' she signed.

Lizzie nodded, but in her head she was already busily making detective plans. The first thing she needed to do was find the farmer, Mr Baron.

'I'm glad the police let you go, Rita,' said Carla as she made her way past Ted and out of the building. 'We have to fight for what we believe in!' she called as she whizzed off on Lightning. 'See you at the sanctuary!'

Lizzie thought Carla's powerchair could go very fast, but it was a bit dangerous when Carla was driving it.

Lucky stayed close to her family as they left the police station. There were lots of people still about, and she didn't want anyone accidentally stepping on her paws.

Ted pointed out Lizzie's dad heading towards them, and Lizzie gave a **huge sigh** of relief. He was so tall they could see his head above the other people's. When he reached them, he wrapped his arms round Auntie Rita in a big bear hug.

Lucky was very glad to see Lizzie's dad too. He scooped Lucky up and tucked her under his arm. Now Lucky's paws were

safe from the feet of people who didn't notice her.

'The car's not far away,' Dad signed, and he took Lizzie's hand.

It was a bit of a squeeze with Rita in the back of the car as well. Lucky chose to sit on Auntie Rita's lap for a cuddle.

'Lucky's such a sweet puppy,' she signed.

Lucky picked up her octopus toy from the seat to show it to her.

Fortunately, it was only a short drive to the Five Freedoms Animal Sanctuary. And there was a welcome surprise waiting for them when they arrived.

CHAPTER 3

Some of the animals from the sanctuary were waiting for them at the wooden gate.

Herbert, the huge brown-and-white cart horse, towered above the other animals. He whinnied excitedly when he saw Auntie Rita get out of the car. Lizzie remembered from previous visits that Herbert had liked apples very much – Auntie Rita had said he'd eat a whole bucketful if she left it too near him.

Next to Herbert was a grey donkey

called Lulu, then two spotted piglets called Kendo and Asta that Lizzie hadn't met before. Gloria the goat was also there, with her two kids called Elmo and Sweet. Five ducks quacked as if they were saying hello, and the turkey flapped his wings as well.

Behind the turkey was a Jersey cow that Lizzie remembered was called Marigold. Marigold now had a calf of her own called Moon. Auntie Rita had texted Lizzie a photo of him when he was just a few days old. Moon nestled in close to his mum and peered shyly at them all through the gaps in the wooden gate. He seemed to be interested in Lucky most of all. She dropped her octopus toy and

Five
Freedoms
Animal Sanctuary

started wagging her tail and play-bowing to him. But then Lucky noticed an elderly dog, who stood up and gave a slow wag of her own tail.

'That's Peggy,' Lizzie signed to Ted, nodding at the dog. 'And she's very friendly.'

Lucky picked up her octopus toy and took it over to show Peggy.

Auntie Rita told them that the animals at the sanctuary knew lots of sign language too, as she used it all the time. 'I think sign language might be easier for animals to understand than speaking,' she added.

Lizzie nodded. She thought so as well. Sign language was so much more visual than speech.

Standing with the animals was a tall woman wearing a pair of muddy wellingtons. She was holding a rabbit in her arms.

'You have rabbits!' Ted said excitedly. 'I've got two rabbits at home. They're called Thumper and Wriggles. They were always escaping until Lizzie helped me build an adventure garden for them. But why do you have rabbits here? I thought the sanctuary was just for rescued farm animals?'

'Rabbits are often farm animals too,' the woman holding the rabbit told him, and Lizzie lipread her. 'Even though they would much rather be living in warrens in the wild and having fun with other rabbits.'

'This is Ona, one of our newest volunteers to help look after the animals here,' Auntie Rita signed, and the woman holding the rabbit smiled.

A man wearing a raggedy dark blue jumper came out of one of the sheds to wave to them.

'And that's Ona's husband, Oberon,'

Auntie Rita told everyone. 'But he prefers to be called O.B.' She fingerspelt the letters O and B.

'Good to have you back home, Rita,' O.B. said. He held up both thumbs.

Peggy sniffed noses with Lucky, but the elderly dog didn't want to play just now. She wanted Auntie Rita to stroke her, so Lucky went back to play-bowing to Moon. The calf play-bowed back on his gangly legs.

Auntie Rita bent down to stroke Peggy. 'I'd happily be arrested a million times if it would stop that chicken megafarm from happening,' she signed.

'Me too!' shouted Carla, bumping over the grass in Lightning to join them.

'But what would happen to the animals here if you were arrested again?' Ted signed to her.

'There's lots of people who'd help look after them,' Ona said. 'Me and O.B. for a start.'

'We'd help look after them too,' Mum signed as she looked over at Dad, who smiled and nodded.

'Of course we would,' he signed back.

Auntie Rita stood up and hugged Mum.

'You're the best little sister,' she signed. 'I hope we can find a way to stop it from happening at all.'

Lizzie nodded. She loved helping at the sanctuary, but she didn't want Auntie Rita to get into any trouble with the police again. She needed to find a better solution to Auntie Rita's problem.

The animals were all very excited to meet Lucky, and she was very happy – if a little bit nervous – to meet them. Lucky followed Auntie Rita closely as she greeted and made a fuss of each of the animals in turn.

Lucky had seen cows in the distance before, but she'd never been so close to one that she could feel its warm breath on her fur, or its soft whiskers tickling her face. Lucky's tail wagged as Marigold gave a gentle **moo**.

'Marigold's talking to Lucky,' Rita signed.

'Talking?' Lizzie signed back with a frown. 'Cows can't talk.'

Ted was nodding. 'She said "*moo*",' he signed.

Rita nodded her head too. 'I saw her neck stretch out and her mouth open – that's how I know. Cows don't talk or sign in the same way we do. But they do communicate with sounds and gestures of their own.'

'Marigold's always talking to her calf, Moon, and giving him licks. She loves Moon more than anything in the whole world,' Carla told them.

'Even more than food?' signed Ted, as

O.B. headed over with a large bucketful of carrots and apples.

'Oh yes – all animals love their babies,' Auntie Rita said.

'Same as all people love their children,' signed Lizzie's dad, and Lizzie's mum smiled and put her arms round Lizzie and Ted.

The fruit and veg were very popular with the animals. Even the ducks ate the little bits Lizzie gave them.

'I never thought I'd be hand-feeding a turkey,' Ted signed after it took a piece of carrot from him.

Lucky liked carrots very much too and crunched away happily when Lizzie gave her one.

Herbert's mouth was warm, and the huge horse's lips tickled Lizzie's hand as he gently took the apple she held out to him.

'Apples are Herbert's favourite.' Auntie Rita signed, and Lizzie nodded.

Three sheep spotted the feast and headed over from the shed where O.B. had been.

'I love how your animals can go wherever they like,' Lizzie signed to Auntie Rita. 'It's like they're really at home here.'

It was one of Lizzie's favourite things about the sanctuary. Even at night, the larger animals could decide for themselves where they'd like to sleep.

Sometimes Herbert liked to sleep outside under the stars and sometimes in his cosy warm shed. One of the pot-bellied pigs, called Priscilla, liked to nap with Lulu the donkey.

Usually everyone chose the same spot to rest in and which other animals to be near, but not always. Once everyone was settled for the night in their various homes, Auntie Rita would check on them all to make sure they were cozy, comfortable and safe.

'You're right, Lizzie. It's lovely that they're free to roam as they please,' signed Lizzie's mum. 'Animals have needs, just like humans.'

'Like the Five Freedoms,' Carla told them.

'What are those?' Ted wanted to know.

Carla listed the five freedoms of the Animal Welfare Act on her fingers:

Freedom from hunger and thirst.
Freedom from discomfort.
Freedom from pain and injury.
Freedom from fear and distress.
Freedom to express normal behaviour.

'All animals should have the chance to live a long, happy life, like the animals here at the sanctuary do.'

Auntie Rita looked very sad. 'I can't bear the thought that the farm next door could have up to a million chickens in its huge barns.'

'A million!' signed Lizzie, and everyone else looked really shocked. It was hard to imagine even a thousand chickens, let alone a million.

Auntie Rita nodded. 'And as soon as Butterbrooks has planning permission, they'll have the barns up in no time, and the farm will open. It could be any day.'

Lizzie shook her head. It wasn't right, not right at all. And she was going to stop it.

CHAPTER 4

Herbert, who'd already crunched his way through a lot of apples and carrots, now started whinnying and stamping his hooves. Auntie Rita looked at her watch and laughed.

'Time for dinner. Herbert likes his meals to be as regular as clockwork,' she signed. 'Plus snacks in between, of course.'

'Same as Lucky,' signed Lizzie.

Lucky knew when it was time for lots of different things besides food. She knew when it was time to get up and time to go to sleep; when it was time for Lizzie to go to school and come home; and when the post was due. But food time was her favourite.

The other animals were getting restless too. Gloria and her two goat kids, Elmo and Sweet, started bleating and butting heads.

'My animals always know when their meals are due, and they don't like to be kept waiting,' Auntie Rita signed.

'We'll help,' signed Mum, and everyone nodded. It wasn't fair to keep the animals from their food.

Lucky was hungry too, and she ate a bowl of the same food as Peggy. Lucky looked up at Lizzie and licked her lips. Then she looked back at her food bowl as if to say, *I wouldn't mind seconds*. Lizzie laughed and gave Lucky a stroke.

Once all the animals had been fed, it was time for Ona, O.B. and Carla to go home, while Lizzie, Lucky and Ted followed Auntie Rita, Mum and Dad past a caravan next to a big pink rose bush and into the house.

When they got inside, the grown-ups started to make a vegan lasagne in Auntie Rita's tiny (and very messy) kitchen. Dad made the sauce by blending up cashew nuts.

'It'll be ready in about an hour,' Mum signed to Lizzie. 'Why don't you show Ted around while we're cooking?'

'Can we go see the rabbits?' signed Ted.

Lizzie nodded, and they headed back outside, past the rose bush and the caravan and down the path.

There were currently six rabbits living at the sanctuary. They were hopping about in their enclosed run, which joined

on to a large rabbit house.

'I bet they'd like an adventure garden like the one we made for my rabbits,' Ted signed, and Lizzie nodded.

'Only theirs could be **even bigger**,' she added.

Lizzie took Lucky and Ted on a mini-tour of the rest of the sanctuary. The chickens, ducks and turkeys all lived together in a large coop. Next to the coop was the pigsty, where Priscilla and another pot-bellied pig called Pumpkin were having a snooze. Then there was the big old greenhouse that had a few tomato plants and lettuces growing in it, but Auntie Rita didn't really use it much.

'That's new,' Lizzie signed, pointing at

a treehouse tucked into the branches of a large oak. The treehouse wasn't very big, but it looked just the right size for Lizzie, Ted and Lucky. It had a ramp going up to it, which they used.

Lizzie wondered if Carla had come up here in Lightning, and thought that she probably had. She imagined Carla racing back down the ramp afterwards.

From the treehouse they could see crops of broccoli and cauliflowers growing in some fields beyond, as well as a field full of sheep and their newborn lambs, and a herd of cows in the distance. Mr Baron certainly did have a lot of land to sell. But what would happen to his sheep and cows then?

'Auntie Rita once told me that the soil here is clay. That means it's not so good for growing crops like wheat,' Lizzie signed. 'But the sheep and cows seem to like the grass growing on it. And it's the perfect soil to find fossils in too.'

Ted's eyes opened wide.

'You mean like dinosaur fossils?' he signed.

Lizzie wasn't sure. Auntie Rita hadn't mentioned dinosaurs, but then Auntie Rita was very focused on her animal family.

'She showed me some small ones by the overgrown pond. I think they're called ammonites,' Lizzie signed.

'**Ammonites?** I read about those in my favourite dinosaur book!' Ted signed back excitedly. 'They can be over four-hundred-million years old!'

Lizzie mouth fell open. She made the sign for **'really?'**

Ted nodded.

Lizzie pointed the pond out to him, but Ted shook his head and made the sign for 'where?' He couldn't see it because it was partially hidden by the tall, thick ferns that grew in the area.

Ted wanted to search for ammonites straight away, so the three of them headed back down the ramp. They went past the rabbit house and the grassy paddock where the sanctuary's animals liked to play.

Half of the pond was on Auntie Rita's

land, and half of it was on the farm next door's side, which belonged to Mr Baron.

Ted was so happy when he found his first ammonite. 'They look like giant snail shells,' he said, examining it with wonder. 'Would Auntie Rita let me keep it?'

'I expect so. We can ask her,' Lizzie signed.

Lucky, who'd been sniffing around the edge of the pond, suddenly went racing towards the stream that led from it. Lizzie could tell she'd spotted something interesting by the way she was jumping about and wagging her tail. Maybe it was a duck or a moorhen.

But when Lizzie headed over to the stream, she couldn't see any birds. What she did see was something swimming away fast. It looked almost like a thick-coated dog, only she knew that couldn't be right. It wasn't a dog . . . **it was an otter!**

She beckoned to Ted to come and see,

but he was too busy looking for more fossils.

Lucky sat down at the side of the stream and stared in the direction that the otter had gone. She wanted to play.

Lizzie had always liked coming to the pond because of the newts with orange-and-black tummies that lived here. Sometimes she'd seen the newts swimming in the water, and a few times she'd seen one sunbathing on the grass. Once she'd even seen one that looked like a tiny dragon with a black crest running along its back. Now there was an otter too, and if there was one there might be more – perhaps even a whole family of otters.

Lizzie and Lucky headed back over to

Ted. He now had the ammonite plus some other, smaller fossils and a rock he liked the look of.

'Better head back soon,' Lizzie signed to Ted, and he nodded. But something made him suddenly spin round.

Lizzie turned too. On the other side of the pond she saw an old, very angry looking man with lots of wild white hair and a long white beard. He was leaning on a walking stick with a gold metal tip.

'What are you two doing here?' the old man asked, and Lizzie lipread him. **'You're trespassing, and you're stealing!'** He nodded at Ted's handful of fossils and the rock.

Lizzie and Ted shook their heads. They

hadn't been doing anything wrong, and this land belonged to Auntie Rita too. Lucky started jumping about and barking – she didn't like the old man.

'Come on,' Ted said to Lizzie, beckoning her away. 'Let's go.'

'That's right, and don't come back!' the old man shouted after them, and Ted translated for Lizzie. 'Stay away from my pond!'

Who was that man? Lizzie wondered. *What was he doing at the pond? And why was he so angry?*

★

When they got back to the sanctuary, Lizzie told Auntie Rita about their encounter.

Ted ran into the dining room to show Lizzie's mum and dad the amazing fossils he'd found.

'Do you think it was the farmer next door, Mr Baron?' Lizzie asked her auntie, who was taking the lasagne from the oven.

'I don't know,' Auntie Rita signed after she'd put the lasagne on the counter. 'I've never met him in all the time I've been here, although I've had written complaints about my sanctuary animals wandering on to his land sometimes.' She frowned and then added, 'I did see a photograph of him once in the newspaper. He looked very distinguished, with dark hair and a handlebar moustache.'

Lizzie thought back to the old man she and Ted had met. He had white hair and a long beard. Maybe he was Mr Baron's father, or another relative?

It was all a bit of a mystery.

Ted came into the kitchen with Lizzie's mum and dad.

When Auntie Rita had admired Ted's fossils, she signed that the pond belonged just as much to her as it did to the farm next door.

'I'll come with you next time,' Dad signed.

'Whoever you met sounds like a bully,' signed Mum.

Lizzie nodded, but she wasn't frightened of bullies.

Lucky was sniffing at the closed lounge door and put her paw out. Lizzie opened the door for her, and there they found three sweet little orphaned kittens playing on the mat with Lucky's octopus toy. Lucky lay down on the mat too, and the kittens crawled all over her. Ted signed

to Lizzie that they were making little mewing noises.

Auntie Rita also had some poorly ducks in her bath, and a sheep and her lamb resting in one of the other rooms.

'There sure are lots of animals at the sanctuary,' Ted signed, and Lizzie nodded.

Dinner was finally ready, and everyone was very hungry. Ted had two platefuls of the vegan lasagne, and he really liked the cashew-nut cheese.

'So full. Thank you,' he signed when he'd finished. He looked down at his empty plate and rubbed his tummy. 'So, so full.'

Lizzie laughed and rolled her eyes. Ted was funny.

'I have some coconut-milk ice cream and strawberries,' Auntie Rita signed, 'if you'd like some dessert.'

Lizzie, who'd thought she was full up too, found she could make a little more space for coconut-milk ice cream, and so could Ted. Lucky had some strawberries.

'We should probably be going soon,' Dad signed, looking at his watch.

Auntie Rita looked sad.

'We can come back tomorrow morning,' Dad promised.

But Auntie Rita didn't want them to leave.

'You could stay here,' she signed. 'I'd like you to. You'd be really welcome.'

Lizzie had never stayed at Auntie Rita's

overnight before because she didn't have much space in the house. But they had been planning to come and stay to help with repainting the animals' homes during the summer holidays. Mum and Dad worked at their local theatre as stage designers and prop makers, and so they were very good at decorating and repairs.

'I suppose we could start our visit now. We're already here after all,' Dad signed, and Mum smiled and nodded.

'I've got the paint ready,' Auntie Rita signed.

Lizzie and Ted looked at each other and grinned.

'I could make an adventure garden for your rescued rabbits,' signed Ted.

'I bet some of the other animals would like one too,' signed Lizzie.

'Will you stay then?' Auntie Rita signed hopefully. 'Maybe for a few days? A week or two would be **even better**.'

Lizzie's mum and dad put their thumbs up. Auntie Rita took Lizzie's mum's hand and smiled, as Ted went into another room to call his gran and ask if he could stay too.

But where would they all sleep? Rita's house was very small, and it was already full of rescued animals who needed extra care.

'You can all stay in the caravan – that's where the volunteers sleep when they need to stay over,' signed Auntie Rita. 'It's a bit basic but perfectly clean and comfortable. Plus it doesn't have any animals in it, unlike my house.'

'My gran said I can stay but she wanted to know what I should do about clean clothes. I only have the ones I'm wearing,' Ted said as he rejoined them. 'And what about toothbrushes?'

'I've got a whole box of new bamboo toothbrushes,' Auntie Rita signed. 'And you can tell your gran that I have spare clothes here, and a washing machine to wash your clothes in if needs be. You don't need to look smart at the sanctuary.'

Ted phoned his gran again to let her know. Ted's gran said she'd look after his rats and rabbits while he was away.

Lucky picked up her octopus toy and gave it a shake. She was happy to stay too. She had her favourite toy and she could share Peggy's delicious meals.

Lizzie smiled at Lucky. She loved visiting Auntie Rita and her animals, and **she had a mystery to solve too**.

CHAPTER 5

It was very late at night, and Lizzie was fast asleep in a sleeping bag on the sofa in the caravan. Auntie Rita had given her a pair of old pyjamas to wear. They were a bit big, but Mum had helped her to roll them up.

Fortunately some of the volunteers had left spare clothes at the sanctuary, and Auntie Rita had managed to find outfits for everyone – even Dad now had a pair of overalls that were big enough for him, thanks to O.B.

Lizzie felt Lucky jump on to the sofa and start tapping at her with a paw. She opened her eyes and smiled. She didn't mind being woken up at all. Before she'd had Lucky, Lizzie used to be frightened at night, and it had been hard for her to fall asleep. She would worry that a burglar would break in and she wouldn't hear them, or that there might be a fire and she wouldn't hear the alarm. But ever since Lucky had come to live with her, she'd fallen asleep almost as soon as her head touched the pillow. Life was much better.

As soon as Lucky saw Lizzie was awake, she jumped off the sofa and headed over to the caravan's front door. There she sat down and looked back at

Lizzie, with her head tilted to one side.

The room was suddenly lit up by a car's headlights, which shone into the room through the thin curtains. Lizzie gasped as the lights cast a strange shadow on the wall – the black shape of a giant beaked creature. Only it wasn't like any animal she'd ever seen – at least not in real life. It was more like . . . **a dinosaur!** Lizzie rubbed her eyes in disbelief. But the next moment, the lights faded and the shadow vanished.

Lizzie breathed a sigh of relief, but Lucky was scratching at the door of the caravan, wanting to go out.

Lizzie was nervous about what they might find outside, but – like any good

detective – she was also curious. She got out of bed, slipped on her shoes, grabbed the torch from her detective bag and carefully opened the caravan's door just a crack. Lucky squeezed past her. There were no giant creatures as far as she could see, and the car had gone too.

Outside, the night sky was full of stars – more stars than Lizzie had ever seen before. She stared up at them. They were so beautiful.

Lucky ran over to the pink rose bush, her tail wagging, and started pawing at something. Lizzie caught up to her, and there she found a big cardboard box.

Lizzie knew it hadn't been there when they'd gone to bed. Had the person in the car with the bright headlights left it? What was in it?

Lucky was sniffing at the box now. Lizzie thought she saw the leaves of the rose bush moving, but when she switched on her torch to check, there was nothing there. The flaps of the cardboard box weren't sealed down, so Lizzie lifted one of them and shone her torch inside.

A pair of small beady eyes stared back at her. Then she saw a second pair of eyes looking up into her own, and a third.

A hand touched Lizzie on the shoulder and made her jump. It was Auntie Rita.

'I saw car headlights,' she signed.

Lizzie nodded and pointed at the cardboard box in the rose bush. 'I think they were left here.'

Lizzie's mum and dad and Ted came out of the caravan too.

'What's going on?'

'Someone's left three chickens here, in this box. We don't know who it was,' Lizzie signed.

Auntie Rita continued. 'It isn't that unusual for people to abandon their animals at sanctuaries. It's better than just leaving them at the side of the road. I've had people anonymously drop off unwanted pets and farm animals. Often the farm animals are sick when they arrive.' She looked into the cardboard box as Lizzie gently shone her torch with her hand half over it so the light wasn't too bright. 'These chickens don't look very well at all.'

Ted looked in the box too. 'What's happened to their feathers?' he signed.

'Sometimes they lose them when they get stressed or sick,' Auntie Rita told him. 'They'll grow back once these chickens are properly looked after.'

Lizzie pulled out a piece of paper from the box. It had thick black marker-pen writing on it.

"Please take care of these four chickens", she read. There was no address or any other information about them at all.

Lizzie held up three fingers and pointed

in the box. There were only three chickens inside it, **not four**.

'Where's the fourth one?' she signed.

Auntie Rita shook her head. Lizzie shone her torch into the rose bush and around the yard, but she couldn't see any more chickens.

'Are they going to be OK?' Ted signed to Auntie Rita. The three chickens were looking very sorry for themselves indeed – one of them couldn't even hold her head up.

'I hope so. We'll have to see how they are in the morning,' Auntie Rita told him.

Lizzie's dad lifted the box from the rose bush and carried the chickens to their new home. He put the box carefully down on the straw-laden floor of one of the smaller sheds that didn't have any other animals in it. But even though Auntie Rita pulled down one side of the box, none of the chickens came out.

'Give them time,' Auntie Rita signed. 'We don't know what their lives were like before. Some egg-laying chickens live their whole lives in cages. They might not know how to be free – but they'll learn.'

She left some food and water close to the birds, and then they all headed off to bed.

'I expect these three will want to explore in the morning,' Auntie Rita signed to Lizzie.

Lizzie hoped so. **But where was the fourth chicken?**

It was another mystery, and Lizzie couldn't wait to solve it.

CHAPTER 6

Lizzie woke up early the next morning and immediately thought of the chickens they'd rescued. The note had said there were four of them. So where was the other one? She picked up her detective bag. **It was time to investigate.**

Lucky wagged her tail. She loved investigating as much as Lizzie did.

The first place they looked for clues was in the rose bush. Lizzie pulled her magnifying glass from her detective bag and examined every inch of the rose bush carefully. Lucky helped by sniffing at the spots where Lizzie looked.

A few minutes later, Lizzie found a potential clue. It was a small strand of dark blue wool. Lizzie used her tweezers to pull it from a rose thorn where it had got caught. The wool looked new, clean and

dry. It couldn't have been in the bushes for very long. Lizzie dropped it into one of her clue bags.

But what did it mean? The wool could have come from the clothing of the person who'd left the chickens in the cardboard box, or it could have come from someone else. They'd all walked past the rose bush on the way to the caravan and back, and O.B. had been wearing a blue jumper yesterday. She would have to compare it to the thread.

Lizzie re-examined the rose bush, but she didn't find any more clues there. What she did spot was the imprint of a tyre track in the grass close to where Lucky was sniffing.

It was too big for Lightning or a bicycle

to have made, and too small for a tractor to have left. The track looked like it had been made by a car. Lizzie took a photograph of it. She could compare the pattern of the treads to the tyres of the other cars at the sanctuary to rule them out as possibilities. She could also see if she could find any more of the tracks at the sanctuary, to show which direction the car might have come from.

She picked up her detective bag. That would do for now. It was time to see if the three chickens from last night had started exploring their new home yet.

★

Lizzie and Lucky headed over to the small shed, but didn't go inside because

Lizzie didn't want to frighten the chickens or wake them up if they were still sleeping.

The shed window was a bit high for Lizzie to look through, so she found a tin bucket and stood on that. Now she could see properly, she saw that the abandoned chickens were still hiding in their box, but the

food Auntie Rita had left for them had been eaten. Lizzie took that to be a **very** good sign.

As she peered through the murky window, Lizzie saw the blurry reflection in the glass of something small and *blue* standing on the path behind her, staring up at her. It was such a surprise that she had to grab the windowsill to stop herself from falling. But when she looked round, whatever it was had already gone.

Lizzie frowned as she stepped off the bucket, picked up her detective bag and headed over to the spot where she had seen it. Whatever it was, it hadn't looked big. It definitely wasn't Peggy or one of the kittens, and it was definitely a strange blue colour. She simply didn't know what she'd seen.

It was true that the glass had been very dirty, but she was sure the creature had been there. Had it been making a sound? She didn't know.

Lizzie crouched down for a closer look, and saw that a few blades of grass had been squashed where the creature had been and some of them were torn through. The earth had also been scuffed in places. Lucky's little nose sniffed and sniffed. But Lizzie couldn't see any footprints, and Lucky's nose didn't find a trail to follow.

After one last look, Lizzie and Lucky headed over to the paddock. All the way there, Lizzie kept looking around in case she spotted the strange creature again. There were so many places for it to have hidden – after all, the sanctuary was a maze of sheds and outbuildings.

The goats were already in the paddock. Elmo and Sweet were chasing each other around and around and jumping about, while their mother, Gloria, chewed on some hay.

Lizzie thought that Elmo and Sweet might like Ted to build them an adventure garden to play in too.

Lucky looked over at the goats and wagged her tail, but she wasn't sure if she could join in their fun. She looked up at Lizzie quizzically.

Lizzie pointed at the goats and made

the sign for **'OK'**. She climbed on to the first rung of the fence gate and watched as Lucky ran over to Elmo and Sweet. Now the three of them were racing around together in a wild game of chase.

They took it in turns to be the chaser, until they were exhausted and lay down in a heap together.

Meanwhile, Lizzie climbed up another two rungs of the fence so that she could better see what was happening at the farm next door.

The sanctuary paddock had an overgrown lane running along it, dividing Auntie Rita's land from Mr Baron's. Two cars and a van were now bumping their way down it.

Lizzie watched as the vehicles stopped, and people got out and started unloading what looked a lot like detective equipment.

Lizzie pulled Lucky's dog whistle from her detective bag and blew on it.

Lucky immediately jumped up and came running over to her, squeezing through the fence. Elmo and Sweet heard the whistle too and ran after Lucky, but their mother Gloria started bleating at them, so they stayed in the field.

Lizzie and Lucky headed over to the lane between the two properties. A friendly looking lady was stretching out some bright yellow tape with the word **CAUTION** written on it.

Lizzie wondered what it could be for. It looked almost as if a crime scene was being marked out, but the people couldn't be the police because they weren't wearing uniforms. Unless they were undercover officers?

Lizzie wanted to ask the lady what she was doing, but she thought the lady probably wouldn't know any sign language – most people didn't. Fortunately, Lizzie had her detective bag with her, and it had a notebook and pencil inside it.

She pulled the notebook out and wrote in it. Then she showed the lady what she had written.

What are you doing?

The lady smiled, and put her index and middle finger to her ear and raised her eyebrows to ask Lizzie if she was deaf.

Lizzie nodded and the lady started to sign fluently. Lizzie was amazed.

'My mum and dad are deaf,' the lady signed. 'I learnt to use sign language before I could even speak.'

Lizzie smiled. Children of deaf adults were called CODAs. That explained why the lady was so fluent.

'My name's Margaret, and I'm an archaeologist, which means I study how

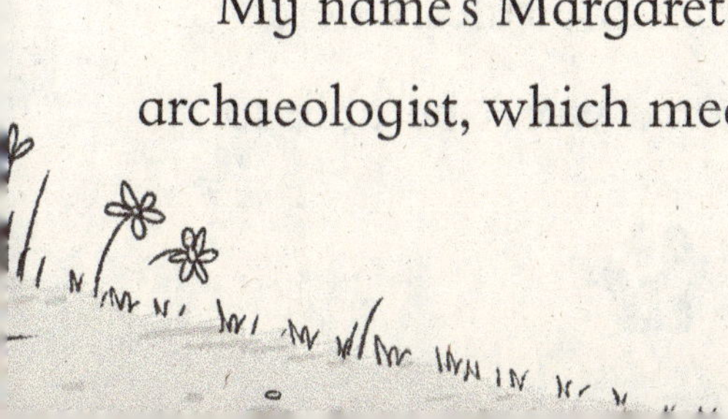

people lived in the past by digging for clues about their lives in the soil. We're going to be making a trench here, and then we'll write down anything interesting we find inside it,' she signed to Lizzie.

Lucky rubbed her head against Margaret's leg, and she gave the puppy a stroke.

'I'm putting this tape up to show everyone exactly where we're going to dig,' Margaret signed to Lizzie. 'Mr Baron, the farmer, is selling his land to a company called Butterbrooks, and they want to build on it as soon as they can, but before they can do that, we need to investigate what's in the soil – it's the rules. There's lots of farmland, so we won't be able to inspect every little bit – that could take years. Not unless we find something really interesting. Then the building work would have to be delayed or even stopped.'

The old man with wild white hair that Lizzie had seen yesterday was heading towards them. He was leaning heavily on

his stick as he walked, and he still looked angry. Lucky barked when she saw him.

'**You again!** What's going on?' he shouted and Lizzie lipread, even though his lips were hard to read because his face was scowling.

'Please ask him if he's Mr Baron,' Lizzie signed to Margaret, pointing at the old man.

Margaret did so and the old man nodded his head. 'That's me – not that it's any of your business.'

'Why are you selling your farmland?' Lizzie signed, and again Margaret translated for her.

Mr Baron frowned as if he didn't want to be questioned, but finally answered

Lizzie. 'If you must know, it's because my daughter, Emilia, and I had a row about it.' Margaret signed what he'd said to Lizzie.

But now Lizzie had even more questions. 'Why did you fall out?' She wanted to know.

Mr Baron frowned. 'She disagreed with me for wanting to sell to Butterbrooks. She didn't want the land to become a chicken farm. I told her it was the best way to make money, and some of that money would be hers one day, but she wouldn't listen. She wanted me to sell it to a fruit and vegetable farmer instead – but I said no. That's when she got angry and stormed out,' Mr Baron told Margaret.

'Did you get in touch with her to say you were sorry?' Lizzie signed and Margaret spoke.

Now Mr Baron looked really angry. 'You're being very nosy. No, I didn't, because I don't know exactly where she is. She went to work in Australia.'

'Where in Australia?' Lizzie signed to Margaret.

'I don't know and I don't care!' Mr Baron shouted. And with that, he stomped off, leaving Lizzie and Lucky staring after him. Lizzie could tell he was lying about not caring about his daughter because he looked very sad.

Could Emilia be the key to stopping Mr Baron from selling the farm? Lizzie

ANIMAL

wondered. Emilia didn't want it to go to Butterbrooks either, so it was definitely worth a try. But there could be lots of Emilia Barons living in Australia, so Lizzie needed more information about her. The first thing to investigate was where in Australia had she moved to.

Fortunately Lizzie had a friend who might be able to help.

Another of the archaeologists came over to them. Her name was Jane and she was holding what looked like a small spade with a pointed tip.

Margaret explained to Lizzie that the process of carefully removing soil and objects from an area of historical interest was called a 'dig'.

‘We use these little trowels so we don’t damage any things we might find, like old pots, or perhaps jewels – although that’s very rare,’ Jane told Lizzie as Margaret

translated.

'Even broken things are good for telling us about the people who might have lived here in the past. Although this clay soil is **even better** for finding fossils,' Jane added.

Lizzie nodded, and signed that there were ammonite fossils over by the pond.

Margaret smiled. 'Thank you for telling me. I'm going to ask my friend, who's a palaeontologist, to have a look at those,' she signed. 'I think he'll be very interested.'

Lizzie's heartbeat quickened. She knew what a palaeontologist was. They studied fossils and different life forms from the past. 'Do you think there might be *dinosaur* fossils here?' she signed. Ted would be so pleased.

Margaret smiled. 'We never know quite what we'll find. That's why this job is so exciting.'

'It's a bit like being a detective,' Lizzie signed, and Margaret nodded.

'It is. Being an archaeologist or a palaeontologist is a lot like being a detective. You follow clues to the past – and sometimes you can even use them to solve a mystery or two.'

CHAPTER 7

Lizzie and Lucky went to find Auntie Rita to tell her about Mr Baron and the dig. But as they headed back towards the abandoned chicken's small shed, Lizzie kept getting the strange feeling that they were being followed. Only when she looked round, she couldn't see anyone, or any*thing,* there. Lucky looked up at her and wagged her tail. She didn't seem to be feeling uncomfortable at all.

Lizzie arrived at the chickens' shed,

and Auntie Rita beckoned them inside. The three chickens weren't in their box any more – they were exploring their new home. One of them still looked a bit confused, but the other two were strutting about and pecking at the straw that lined the floor.

Lucky sat down and watched them.

'Could you please go and open the door to the outside?' Auntie Rita signed to Lizzie.

Lizzie did so very gently, and the morning sunshine flooded in.

Auntie Rita gave Lizzie some corn for the chickens, which she scattered outside on the grass. First one chicken came out and started pecking at the food, and then another, and finally the third joined them.

Their feet trod carefully on the unfamiliar ground.

'They've probably never walked on grass before,' Auntie Rita said. 'Judging by how they're behaving, I think they've always lived in cages and couldn't even spread their wings. They're not frightened of Lucky – as most chickens would be – and I think that's because they've never seen a dog. That means they won't be

aware of predators, like foxes, at all.'

Lucky stayed close to Lizzie and didn't try to taste the chickens' food, even though she was feeling hungry.

Soon all three chickens were exploring and pecking at bits of grass. The chicken with the poorly neck was holding her head up properly now, and they all seemed to be doing much better.

'I'm going to call her Bunty,' Auntie Rita signed. 'And that one is Grace, because she's so graceful when she steps carefully on the grass.'

'What about the other one?' Lizzie asked, pointing at the third chicken.

'Would you like to give her a name?' Auntie Rita signed back.

Lizzie nodded. None of the chickens had many feathers and she could see their skin underneath those they did have. They were very thin but all of them had good appetites and were pecking at anything interesting they found. These chickens were survivors, and suddenly Lizzie knew just what the third chicken should be called. It was the name of one of the girls in her class.

'Tesha,' she fingerspelt. 'It means "survivor".'

Auntie Rita smiled and signed that Tesha was a perfect name.

Ted came over to say that he'd already started on the rabbits' adventure garden with O.B., and that breakfast was nearly ready. He also told Lizzie and Rita that the chickens were making happy clucking sounds.

Lizzie grinned and held two thumbs up, and Auntie Rita brushed away a tear.

'This is why I do this,' she signed. 'Look at them. They're now free to live the lives they were always supposed to.'

Lizzie watched as Bunty started scratching in the grass. Grace saw what Bunty was doing and copied her. Tesha found a bit of soft, dry earth under a bush and lay down in it, and then wriggled around and had a dust bath, flapping the few wing feathers she had. Bunty and Grace were very interested in Tesha's dust bath and wanted to give it a try too.

Lizzie, Ted and Auntie Rita headed back into the house for breakfast.

'Do you think any other animals here would like an adventure garden too?' Ted signed, and Auntie Rita nodded.

'I think Elmo and Sweet would love one,' Lizzie signed, and Ted grinned.

'I've seen chickens competing in mini

agility courses,' Auntie Rita told them. 'It was really amazing. They are so clever.'

Lizzie frowned as she remembered one of the mysteries she was trying to solve. 'What about the fourth chicken that was supposed to be with the other three in the box?' she signed. 'The note said there were four – so where's the other one gone? I looked by the rose bush for clues earlier, but only found a piece of wool and a car track. It's not enough to go on.' She still needed to check the wool thread against O.B.'s jumper, and her photo of the tyre marks against the cars at the sanctuary.

'Maybe whoever left the chickens here changed their mind and kept it?' Ted signed.

Lizzie nodded – that could be the answer. But she wasn't sure that Ted was right. She needed to investigate more.

Lucky sniffed the air. She could smell tasty food cooking.

Lizzie was glad that the feeling of being followed had gone. She must have been imagining it.

Mum, Dad and Peggy were in the kitchen when they went inside the house. Peggy was sitting next to her food bowl, waiting patiently, and Lucky sat down next to it too. Mum picked up Peggy's bowl and then took out another bowl for Lucky and filled them both with dog biscuits and gravy. It was gone in no time. Lucky sniffed again and licked her lips as

more delicious smells wafted towards her.

Mum and Dad had made blueberry pancakes with oat milk and flour for their breakfast. They used ground flaxseeds mixed with water instead of eggs.

'Yum!' Ted signed after he bit into one.

Lizzie took a mouthful of her blueberry pancake and then cut off a bit to give to Lucky.

Over breakfast, Lizzie told everyone about the archaeologists' dig at the farm next door.

'A palaeontologist is going to be looking at the pond too,' she signed.

Ted was so excited he almost spat out his pancake.

‘A palaeontologist! Do you think they might find a dinosaur fossil?’ he signed.

‘Maybe,’ Lizzie replied.

‘The soil around here is famous for fossils,’ signed Auntie Rita.

Ona and O.B. came into the kitchen, and Dad made them a cup of tea while Mum cooked some more pancakes. O.B. was wearing the same dark blue jumper he’d worn yesterday, but even without her magnifying glass Lizzie could tell the wool she’d found in the rose bush was different. O.B.’s sweater was made from a thick, chunky wool, whereas the thread in the rose bush had been much finer. She took the thread from her detective bag and looked at it just to be sure. The colours were similar but definitely not the same. It was a dead end.

O.B. caught her staring at him and looked down at his jumper and then up at her.

'Did I spill something on it?' he asked with a grin.

Lizzie shook her head as she lipread him and then signed that she'd found a thread of dark blue wool in the rose bush and wondered if it came from his jumper, or the person who dropped the chickens off. Ted translated for her.

'Lizzie, I'm not sure it matters *who* brought the birds to us in the car. What's important now is that we take care of Bunty, Grace and Tesha, and find the lost one too,' Auntie Rita signed.

Lizzie nodded. Perhaps Auntie Rita was right. She would ignore the photo of the car tracks from her camera, but was determined to find the fourth chicken.

Ted started telling O.B. about the exciting palaeontologist news.

'Who knows what they'll find. It could even be a dinosaur fossil,' he said, with a happy smile of anticipation.

Lizzie was looking forward to seeing what the palaeontologist found too. But she was also worried that even if they found a whole giant dinosaur skeleton fossil, it might not be enough to stop Butterbrooks's chicken farm from happening. Once Mr Baron had done his deal with them, it would be too late.

She needed to find Mr Baron's daughter, Emilia, and ask her to help. He'd seemed sad that they'd fallen out, so maybe he'd listen to her this time.

Australia was a very big country and she didn't know where Emilia was living.

But Australian Sign Language, or Auslan as it was known, was very similar to British Sign Language, and Lizzie's class had teamed up with a school for Deaf children in Sydney. Instead of pen pals, they had online signing friends. Lizzie's signing friend in Australia was called Nora and her dad was a police officer. Maybe they could help.

It was time to bring in reinforcements and investigate more.

CHAPTER 8

It was a beautiful day, so after breakfast everyone went outside. The goats, Elmo, Sweet and Gloria, were with the piglets, Kendo and Asta, in the paddock, and Lucky wanted to play with all of them.

First they played chasing each other. But then Lizzie took Lucky's ball from her detective bag. When she threw it, they all excitedly ran after it. Even Moon the calf and his mother, Marigold, came out of the cowshed to join in.

Mum and Dad headed past with brushes and pots of paint. It was time for Herbert and Lulu's stable to be transformed. They smiled at Lizzie before going inside.

Suddenly, out of the corner of her eye, Lizzie thought she saw something small scuttle out of the shadows of the stable door and follow her mum and dad inside. Lizzie rubbed her eyes. She couldn't be sure, and it didn't make any sense, but it looked like it was wearing *clothes*.

Lizzie ran after her mum and dad and into the stable. Herbert and Lulu were outside in the sunshine.

'OK?' Mum signed when she saw Lizzie.

'I thought I saw something small following you,' Lizzie signed. But there didn't seem to be anyone here besides Mum and Dad.

'Maybe it was a rat?' Dad signed.

Lizzie shook her head. *No, it definitely*

hadn't been a rat, I'm sure of that. Maybe it was just a trick of the light, she told herself, as she headed back to the paddock, although she knew in her heart that it wasn't.

Once Lucky had had a good play and the piglets and goats were ready for a nap, Lizzie picked up her detective bag, and she and Lucky went to find Ted.

He wasn't in the caravan or the house, and Lizzie knew he wasn't helping Mum and Dad to redecorate the cowshed because he hadn't gone past the paddock. They headed over to the rabbits.

But he wasn't there either – although Lizzie could see he'd been busy making their adventure garden. It was looking good so far, and she was sure the rabbits would love playing in it.

'Where's Ted?' Lizzie signed to Lucky. Lucky was very good at finding people. It was one of the things she and Lizzie practised a lot. Sometimes she'd find people just by the smell of their clothes. Lucky had found Ted lots of times before, even when he'd been hiding in hard-to-find places.

Now Lucky sniffed the air and followed a trail of scent along the ground with her nose. Then she went running over to the tall oak tree at the end of the paddock, wagging her tail. She looked back at Lizzie and then up at the tree.

Lizzie saw Ted waving at her from

the top of it. Of course – he was in the treehouse! It was such a leafy tree that if he crouched down no one would know he was up there – not even if they were standing close by.

Ted beckoned to them to join him, and Lizzie and Lucky went up the ramp. Ted told her O.B. had built the treehouse.

'I'd like to help him if he decides to build another one,' Ted signed.

Lizzie nodded. Ted loved making things. Instead of always needing to fingerspell the letters of their name, some Deaf people and sign-language users had special sign names, which often meant using a sign with a different meaning to represent themselves. Ted's sign name was 'make' because that's what he liked to do.

Lizzie's mum's sign name was 'sparkle', and her dad's was 'strong'. Lizzie's own sign name was 'detective' and Lucky's was 'help'.

'O.B. only finished the treehouse last week,' Ted signed.

'It's perfect,' Lizzie signed back.

They looked out at the countryside beyond. Ted spotted a deer in the distance, and Lizzie looked through her binoculars to get a closer look. There were so many birds and butterflies, and even two wild hares hopping about in the grass below.

It was so beautiful, and it made Lizzie feel sad because she knew the pollution from Butterbrooks's chicken farm would hurt the wildlife. Everything around there would change once it was built.

Lizzie was determined to help Auntie Rita. She just wasn't sure how yet. But she'd found Mr Baron, and she hoped finding Emilia would make a difference. She also thought that the treehouse could be a really good place to see what was going on at the farm next door without being noticed – especially if she used her binoculars. She might even spot her next big clue.

CHAPTER 9

It was after lunch, and Lucky was having a nap while Dad was browsing online on Auntie Rita's laptop.

'What time is it in Sydney, Australia?' Lizzie signed to her dad.

'Late. Very late,' he signed back when he'd checked on the internet. 'Two o'clock in the morning.'

Lizzie sighed. It was too late to call Nora for a live sign-chat now, but she could leave her a video message. She switched her phone camera on and started signing. Fortunately Nora loved solving mysteries almost as much as she did.

Dad watched her signing to her friend. 'I can help with finding this Emilia too. It'll be easy-peasy to find someone using the internet,' he told her. 'Where in Australia does she live?'

But Lizzie didn't know where. 'That's

part of the mystery,' she signed back. 'I don't think even her dad, Mr Baron, knows.'

'When was she born?' Dad signed.

Lizzie didn't know that either. Although she knew she was a grown-up.

Dad busily typed away on the computer.

'Maybe I should be a detective too,' he laughed.

The next moment, the light on Lizzie's phone started flashing. It was Nora. She looked very sleepy but also very excited. Nora was holding a pencil and a notebook with a koala bear on the front of it – all ready to take some notes.

Lizzie signed that she was sorry she

woke her up, but Nora shook her head passionately and signed that it was fine. It was important, and she wanted to help.

While Dad looked on the internet for Mr Baron's daughter, Lizzie and Nora sign-chatted. Nora had more questions.

'How long ago did Emilia come to Australia?'

'In the last year I think,' Lizzie signed back.

'Do you know what her job is?'

Lizzie shook her head. 'But I'll try to find out.'

'OK, I'll work on this and get back to you if I have more questions,' Nora signed, and she clicked off.

Just then Lucky woke up, trotted over to Lizzie's detective bag and put her head in, looking for her octopus toy. When she bit on to it and pulled it out, the wildlife crime information leaflet Lizzie had been given on her school trip to the police station was also in Lucky's mouth. Lizzie took it from her and was about to put it back in her bag when something on the front of the leaflet caught her eye. The information was very interesting, and she thought it might come in useful in this case.

Auntie Rita poked her head round the door. 'Lizzie, would you mind putting some fresh straw in one of the slightly larger empty sheds? I want to give the new chickens a little bit more space now they're feeling a bit better,' she signed. 'Bunty, Grace and Tesha are very much enjoying their freedom.'

Lizzie nodded, and she and Lucky ran over to the sheds to do as Auntie Rita had asked. Dad went to help Mum and Ted.

Lizzie had half-finished laying the floor with fresh straw when she saw Lucky sniffing and pawing at a cardboard box in one corner of the shed. It was the box that the three rescue chickens had arrived in.

Lizzie gasped when she saw a small, strange creature peeping out from behind it. The creature had wrinkly blue-black

skin, a blue beak and intelligent brown eyes that stared intently at her. And it was wearing some kind of blue covering or cloak.

Lizzie's heart started to beat very fast, but she knew she had to stay calm.

Holding her hands out in front of her so the strange creature wouldn't be too scared, Lizzie headed towards it. But the next second it had vanished.

Lizzie looked behind the box, but it wasn't there. All she found was lots of old animal rights protest signs. *What was going on? Where could the creature have gone? Why was it wearing a cloak?*

Lucky ran round the shed, sniffing at different spots. But then she came back to sit in front of Lizzie with her head tilted to one side. She looked like she was wondering what sort of creature it was too.

Mum, Dad and Ted had finished painting Herbert and Lulu's stables and came to see how Lizzie and Lucky were getting on.

'They've painted a picture of Herbert and Lulu on the door, but they've given them wings like Pegasus from Greek mythology!' Ted signed to Lizzie. Then he noticed the weird look on Lizzie's face. 'Are you OK, Lizzie?'

Lizzie shook her head and started telling them about the strange creature she'd seen. 'It was standing on two legs and wearing a cloak . . .' But even before she'd finished, she could see they didn't really believe her. In fact, they were trying hard not to laugh.

'You must be so tired – we were all up very late last night,' Mum signed. 'It's hard to sleep properly somewhere different.'

'The light can play tricks on your eyes,' signed Dad.

Lizzie shook her head. She **had** seen something. She knew she had. Just like the other times she'd nearly seen it. Next time she was going to try and take a photograph – then they'd see.

Rita came into the shed with a poultry waterer and feeder, but she didn't know what the strange creature could be either, or if it was even real.

'None of the animals here wear clothing,' she signed, when she'd put the waterer and feeder down. She attached six little chicken-sized cups to the waterer for the chickens to drink from.

Mum pointed at the protest placards

stacked in the corner of the shed.

'Remember how in the old days we used to go on marches all the time to try and make animals' lives better?' she signed to her sister.

Rita nodded.

'Are animals' lives better now than back then?' Lizzie signed.

Rita sadly shook her head. 'Mostly not –

although I'm doing everything I can to help.'

Lizzie smiled and signed Auntie Rita's sign name. It was 'animal helper' and it fitted her perfectly.

Mum laughed and signed that her sister had always been the same.

'She'd put birds back in nests, brought stray animals home to stay . . .' Mum remembered with a smile.

'I just want to protect all creatures and make their lives better,' Auntie Rita signed.

'Thank you for the all the animals you've helped,' Lizzie signed, and Auntie Rita hugged her.

CHAPTER 10

The next day the air was damp with early morning dew as Lizzie and Lucky headed over to see how the dig was getting on. They passed Ted and O.B., who were already in the paddock making a play course for the animals. But it was too early for Margaret and the other archaeologists to have arrived for work yet.

Lizzie found the long trench they'd dug up, still marked off by the yellow tape. There was earth on either side of it, but she couldn't see any artefacts in the overturned soil.

Suddenly Lucky started jumping around and barking. Lizzie looked up and saw Mr Baron.

'I hope you're not here to pinch anything,' he said.

Lizzie lipread him and shook her head firmly. She would never ever steal anything.

'Don't expect they've found anything unusual anyway,' he added, and Lizzie signed that she didn't know.

'I don't understand sign language,' the old man said, and he started to walk off.

Just because she was deaf and he didn't know any sign language didn't mean they

CAUTION
CA

couldn't communicate. Lizzie ran after Mr Baron and touched his arm. She pulled her phone from her detective bag and wrote in the Notes app that a palaeontologist was coming to look too.

'A fossil hunter, hey?' the old man said, and Lizzie lipread him. 'That's very interesting. I've found many ammonites and other small fossils myself by the pond, over the years.' Mr Baron looked down at his walking stick, tapping it into the soil.

'I always wanted to be a palaeontologist you know – ever since I was a boy, but my father wouldn't let me. He wanted me to concentrate on running the farm. I always did what I was told when I was your age and didn't question it. Not like you, or my daughter for that matter. I thought it was the right thing to do. Only, now I feel –' he looked at Lizzie with a desperate look – 'I think I was foolish not to think for myself and make my own decisions. Now I worry I might have wasted my life.'

Lizzie shook her head. He could still do something good. He could still stop the megafarm from happening.

'Don't sell to Butterbrooks,' she typed quickly into the app. **'Please.'**

Mr Baron read what she had written, but he only shook his head sadly. Before Lizzie could type more, he turned away and walked off.

*

Lizzie and Lucky went back to the paddock to tell Ted about what she had just learnt, but he wasn't with O.B. any more. Lizzie thought he might be in the treehouse, so she signalled for Lucky to head up the ramp with her. Ted wasn't there either, but Lizzie thought she might be able to spot him from up high. She could see the pond and the stream from the treehouse too. She took her binoculars from her detective bag to take an even closer look.

Lucky was also looking out. Suddenly she jumped up and raced back down the ramp. Lizzie watched from the treehouse as Lucky ran through the ferns and towards the pond. Lizzie remembered Ted telling her that ferns had been on Earth even before the first dinosaurs had arrived. They were one of the first big plants to grow on land, and it was their oxygen that made the land ready for other life – like the dinosaurs, and eventually people.

For a moment her heart skipped a beat as she couldn't see Lucky any more, but then she breathed a sigh of relief when the puppy came out of the ferns close to the stream. Then, Lizzie's eyes widened in amazement as she saw an otter come out of the water and touch noses with the puppy. She pulled her digital camera from her bag to take a photo of the two of them. Lucky stayed on the stream bank, but the otter darted in and out of the water as the two animals played happily together.

Lizzie smiled. Lucky had made another new friend.

The sun glistened on the water. On

the bed of the stream, Lizzie spotted something. It was even clearer to see with her binoculars and from her vantage point high up in the treehouse. Lizzie was sure – or nearly sure – that what she was looking at was a **HUGE**, three-toed footprint in the stream's clay soil! Might it have been left there by a real dinosaur, millions of years ago?

Lizzie hurried down the treehouse ramp to find out if Margaret's palaeontologist friend had arrived at the site yet. He had to see this. He needed to know what she'd discovered.

The archaeological team had just arrived. Margaret was getting out of the van as Lizzie ran up to her. She smiled at Lizzie.

'Is your palaeontologist friend here too?' Lizzie signed. 'I have something exciting to show him.'

Margaret looked round to see if she could see him. Then she nodded and pointed into the distance at a man with long, plaited hair. He was standing next to the tea and coffee van. 'His name's Ivan,' Margaret signed.

Lizzie was about to run over to him, but Margaret signed to her to wait because Ivan didn't know any sign language.

She handed Lizzie her trowel that she had just taken out of her van. 'I'll translate for you.'

Lizzie nodded and made the sign for 'thank you'. It would be much quicker to communicate with Ivan if Margaret was there too.

Ivan was very interested indeed in what Lizzie had seen and wanted her to show him exactly where.

Lizzie led him and Margaret up the treehouse ramp and pointed to the **giant-sized** three-toed footprint in the stream's clay soil. It was easier to spot from a distance than close up, especially using Lizzie's binoculars.

Ivan touched Lizzie on the shoulder and held up two thumbs. Then he started talking very quickly – too quickly for Lizzie to lipread. But fortunately Margaret was there to translate.

'He thinks you're right Lizzie. It might belong to a dinosaur, and there might be a trail of them, not just one. This could be an amazing find, Lizzie – an amazing find!' Margaret signed. But then Margaret stopped signing and looked shocked instead.

Lizzie looked too – a bulldozer was driving over to the water, and it then started to dig up the soil surrounding the overgrown pond.

Ivan raced down the treehouse ramp, yelling and waving his arms at the other archaeologists and palaeontologists. They dropped their tools and came running over to him.

'What's happening?' Lizzie signed to Margaret.

Margaret shook her head. 'I don't know exactly, but all that digging could easily damage the pond, and cover the dinosaur footprints up if it's filled in. We must try and stop it.' Margaret and Lizzie raced after Ivan.

As they ran, Lizzie thought it wasn't just the dinosaur footprints that mattered but all the creatures that lived in the pond. They'd have nowhere to live if it was filled in.

When they got to the pond, Ivan ran in front of the bulldozer with his arms stretched out to stop it. The driver pulled on the brake and turned the engine off. Lizzie started to take photos of the scene with her digital camera.

Margaret signed to Lizzie what Ivan and the bulldozer driver were saying.

Ivan spoke first. 'This is a very important historical site that needs to be excavated with the utmost care.'

The bulldozer driver just shook his head and shrugged. 'I'm just doing what I'm paid to do,' he said.

'But there's dinosaur footprints here! They might be millions of years old. This could be an incredible find.'

Dinosaurs didn't seem to be enough to stop the bulldozer man. 'You'll have to get in touch with the farmer if you want to stop me,' he said, and he switched the engine back on.

The other archaeologists and

palaeontologists ran in front of the bulldozer and stood there, blocking its way.

Ivan pulled out his phone and waved it in the air. 'I'm calling the police!' he shouted. At that, the bulldozer driver switched the engine off again.

'No need for that,' he said. 'No skin off my nose if the pond is filled in or not.' And with that the bulldozer driver strode off, leaving his machine behind.

'We have to talk to the farmer,' Ivan said. 'He can't get away with destroying history from millions of years ago. It can't be allowed.'

Lucky came running over to Lizzie, and Lizzie leant down and gave her a stroke,

but she was very worried. Lizzie watched as Margaret hurried away with the other adults. Lucky looked towards the stream-side ferns, where a strange blue creature was peeping out and watching them all.

CHAPTER 11

All the outdoor animals had been fed, and it was soon to be Lucky's dinner time. She and Peggy were waiting in the kitchen again, next to their bowls, when suddenly someone knocked at Auntie Rita's door.

A moment later, Auntie Rita led a worried-looking woman inside.

'Hello, I'm Jennifer May,' the woman said as Lizzie lipread. 'I work as Chester Baron's part-time assistant and secretary.

I'm sorry to bother you all, but I don't know what to do. Chester's been missing for hours – ever since those people from the dig came to the house and started shouting about dinosaurs and footprints.'

Jennifer took a deep steadying breath

and continued. 'Chester's a sensitive man, but they didn't seem to care about that. He can't have gone far as he was only on foot, but I've looked everywhere I can think of. He's very old and not as strong as he thinks. I've called the police, but I thought maybe you might be able to help, seeing as you know the area better.'

'We'll help you find him,' Lizzie's dad signed and Ted translated.

'All I've found so far was his handkerchief lying on the ground,' Jennifer said.

'May I borrow it?' Lizzie signed, holding out her hand.

Jennifer gave the handkerchief to her, and Lizzie got Lucky to sniff it. Then she made the sign for 'find'. Lucky wagged her tail because she loved playing finding games.

Lizzie just had time to grab her detective bag and head after Lucky as she ran out of the house. Lucky smelt the air, turning her head one way and then the other. Lizzie offered Lucky the handkerchief to sniff again.

Lucky headed towards the ferns. Some of them were so big that they were taller than Lizzie. They brushed against her face and tugged at her hair as she pushed her way through them. She couldn't see Lucky anywhere, so she scrabbled in her detective bag to find Lucky's dog whistle. The puppy always came back when she blew it.

But before Lizzie could pull the whistle from her bag, she almost stumbled over the little dog. Lizzie gasped.

Lucky was sitting next to Chester Baron. The old man was lying on the ground. Lizzie touched him on the shoulder, and his eyes briefly flickered open before closing again.

‘Find Dad,’ Lizzie signed to Lucky, and Lucky went racing off again to find him.

Lizzie pulled her phone from her detective bag and texted the 999 BSL app. Then she sat down next to the old man in the ferns and held his hand. The 999 BSL interpreter appeared on the screen and signed that she’d send Lizzie’s location to the ambulance service.

Lizzie breathed a sigh of relief when she saw the ferns moving, and then her dad's head appeared. Lizzie waved at him and Lucky.

Dad knelt down next to Chester Baron and checked him over. 'He has a pulse and he's breathing, but he's not conscious and he's very cold,' Dad signed.

The 999 BSL interpreter on Lizzie's phone looked worried. The ambulance wouldn't arrive for a few more minutes yet. They gave Dad instructions on how to keep Mr Baron safe, so Dad took off his jacket and put it over Chester, and then held his wrist to count his pulse.

Lizzie held her phone so Dad could see it, and also so the 999 BSL interpreter could see Dad and give him advice. The 999 BSL interpreter told Lizzie that it was a very good sign when colour started coming back to Chester's cheeks.

A few moments later, a man and woman in ambulance crew uniforms hurried through the ferns with a stretcher. Lizzie jumped up and waved with both hands when she saw them. The old man was now breathing a bit more evenly, though he still wasn't awake. The paramedics lifted Chester carefully on to the stretcher, and told the 999 BSL interpreter that Chester was fortunate to be alive. The interpreter signed their thanks to Dad and Lizzie. Without their help, Chester Baron may not have survived.

Dad hugged Lizzie to him, and they went back to the house with Lucky trotting along beside them.

CHAPTER 12

A few days later, Lizzie and her dad went to the hospital. Lucky really wanted to go in too, but she wasn't allowed, so Mum let Lucky sit on her lap in the car and gave her lots of strokes while they waited.

Lizzie held her dad's hand as the nurse led them to Chester Baron's room. His part-time assistant, Jennifer, was there too, and so was the hospital interpreter. Mr Baron still looked very pale but much better than he had done when they'd rescued him.

'I'm told I have you to thank for saving my life,' the old man said to Lizzie and Dad.

'It was lucky that my puppy, Lucky, found you,' Lizzie signed, and the hospital interpreter spoke for her.

'I wanted to see the dinosaur footprints for myself. I can't believe I've never noticed them before, but the pond did almost dry out earlier in the summer because of all the hot weather we've had. That must be why the tracks showed up.' He smiled a little at Lizzie. 'How can I repay you, young lady?' Chester asked them. 'You must be rewarded. I have lots of money, and I'll have even more, once I've sold my land.'

Lizzie pulled a face. She and Dad didn't want his money. They wanted something much more important.

'Please don't sell your farmland to Butterbrooks,' Lizzie signed, and the interpreter told Chester what Lizzie wanted.

The old man sadly shook his head. 'I'm sorry, but it's too late. The papers are being signed this afternoon. One of Butterbrooks's solicitors is bringing them to the hospital. He's on his way right now. The sale has already been delayed for far too long, and they can't wait any longer. The first of the chicks have already been ordered and are on their way to my farm.'

Dad shook his head in despair, but

Lizzie had one more possible solution – to delay the farm's sale instead.

'We caught your bulldozer trying to fill in the wildlife pond – and it has great crested newts in it, the ones with orange tummies covered in black spots,' she signed and the interpreter translated.

Mr Baron frowned.

Lizzie took out her digital camera to show him the photos of the bulldozer that she'd taken. 'Plus, there's an otter living in the stream. Both of those creatures are protected by law, and building work has to stop immediately when great crested newts are found.'

Now Mr Baron looked shocked. 'I didn't ask for the pond to be filled in,'

he said, as he ran his hand through his wild white hair. 'I love looking at the ammonites there. Did I give that order, Miss May? I don't remember doing so.'

Jennifer wasn't so sure. 'You did say to remove any and all obstacles before the sale. Perhaps one of your staff took it a little too far,' she said.

'I didn't know anything about great crested newts being in the pond,' Chester said. 'Those people that stormed into my house the other day kept shouting about dinosaurs – not wildlife.'

'Damaging a wildlife-protected habitat is a crime and should be reported by calling 999,' Lizzie signed, pulling the leaflet about wildlife crime from her detective bag and handing it to him. 'The punishment is an unlimited fine and up to six months in prison.'

'I can't go to prison!' Chester said, turning pale. He looked at Lizzie and gave a big sigh. 'All right. You win. I won't sign the papers if you promise not to show those photos to the police.'

Lizzie nodded. No actual damage had been done to the pond by the bulldozer. Dad squeezed Lizzie's hand. They'd done it! They had to let Auntie Rita know the good news.

'But Mr Baron,' Jennifer said, looking worried. 'You agreed that the first of the chicks for Butterbrooks could arrive today – even before the sale's officially gone through.'

'Well then, send them back,' Chester told her.

Jennifer picked up her phone and tried to cancel the delivery, but it was too late. She could cancel future

chicks that had been ordered, but the first batch were on their way, and those couldn't be returned.

'The chicks have already left. They told me they'll die if you don't take them,' Jennifer said, and the interpreter translated her words for Lizzie and Dad. 'The journey to your farm and then back again will be too long for the tiny chicks to survive without food or water.'

Lizzie shook her head – they couldn't let that happen. Auntie Rita had told her no animal in need would ever be turned away.

'The Five Freedoms Sanctuary will look after them,' she signed. 'Leave it to us.'

CHAPTER 13

Lizzie and her dad ran out of the hospital and set off in the car with Lucky and Mum. They had to let Auntie Rita know right now that Chester wasn't selling his farm to Butterbrooks any more, but the first batch of chicks that would have been living there were on their way to her sanctuary.

'We'll need to find permanent, happy homes for them,' Auntie Rita signed when she heard what had happened. 'But they can stay here until we do. They're just tiny fluffy yellow babies, so they will need special food and to be kept warm.'

'We could put them in the greenhouse?' Lizzie signed, and Auntie Rita nodded. It was a good plan – the big old greenhouse would do as a short-term place for the chicks, as it was big enough for them and already warm from the hot sunny days. Plus, it had electricity so Auntie Rita could make it even warmer if need be during the night.

But first they'd need to double-check it was secure and then lay fresh straw on the ground. Lizzie, Lucky and Ted went to the greenhouse to make a start, while Mum, Dad and Auntie Rita went to the house

to begin letting people know about the chicks needing homes.

'Make sure there aren't any holes near the ground that the chicks could escape through,' Auntie Rita signed as she left the greenhouse, and Lizzie and Ted began carefully checking every spot.

Lucky sniffed everywhere to make sure there weren't rats that could hurt the chicks.

'I'm so happy that we figured out how to stop Butterbrooks,' Lizzie signed. 'Though we still haven't solved the mystery of the lost chicken. I wonder where it is?'

But Ted wasn't listening. His mouth was wide open, and his eyes had gone very big. His hand shook as he pointed over to a corner. He was pointing at the weird two-legged creature Lizzie had seen before.

'That's the creature I keep seeing!' Lizzie signed.

'What is it? It sort of looks like a tiny dinosaur,' he replied.

When it realized it had been spotted, the creature began to scuttle away, but then it stopped at the greenhouse door and stared back at Lizzie. Lizzie felt as if it was sizing her up, deciding whether to trust her or not.

Just for a second, Lizzie thought the creature really *could* be a tiny dinosaur – maybe a miniature T-rex. But that would be impossible! Could it be a baby one? And why was it wearing clothes? She had so many questions.

As she was thinking, the creature slowly came over to Lizzie. Lizzie held her hand out, and it nudged it with its head. Now she could see it up close, Lizzie realized it wasn't a dinosaur at all, but a blueishblack-skinned bird with no feathers at all that was wearing a blue knitted cloak. That explained the piece of wool she had found in the rose bush.

She knelt down next to it and made the sign for 'bird' to Ted.

Lucky came over to sniff at the potential new friend. The bird didn't seem to be frightened of her at all.

At that moment, Carla came whizzing into the greenhouse on Lightning, followed by Auntie Rita. The bird was very frightened of Lightning and snuggled close to Lizzie for protection.

Once Lightning stopped, the bird peeped out and stared at Carla. Carla smiled back. 'I came to help set up the chicks' new home. Oh, look at that one, it's so sweet,' she said.

Auntie Rita knew right away exactly what the creature was.

'She's a Silkie chicken,' she signed. 'They have blue skin, and normally they have the most beautiful soft, fluffy feathers. . .'

But this Silkie chicken didn't have any feathers. Lizzie could only see the blueishblack skin underneath her knitted cloak. The blue Silkie chicken strutted over to Carla.

'What happened to her feathers?' Ted asked.

Auntie Rita wasn't sure. 'Maybe she was ill,' she signed. 'Or maybe she got very stressed. What I do know is that Silkies are a very friendly breed of chicken, and most of them love cuddles.'

Carla held her hands out to the bird and then leant out of Lightning to pick her up. The little chicken seemed very happy sitting on Carla's lap and looking at them all.

'I think she likes being high up,' Lizzie signed.

'I'm her perch,' said Carla, laughing.

'We should call her Rosie,' signed Lizzie.

'Why?'

'Because of the rose bush the cardboard box was thrown into that she must have escaped from. Rosie's the fourth chicken!' Lizzie signed. 'That's why I kept seeing her around the sanctuary. She was lost and looking for her friends.' Suddenly Lizzie remembered the giant shadow on the caravan wall. It must have been Rosie. The car headlights had made her shadow look **huge**!

Rosie sat on Carla's lap as they headed over to the other three abandoned chickens. It was time for them all to be reunited.

Bunty, Tesha and Grace were very, very pleased to see Rosie. They came racing over as soon as they saw her. Rosie hopped off Carla's lap even before she had a chance to put her down and went running to them. Bunty, Tesha and Grace started dancing around Rosie with joy.

Ted told Lizzie that there were lots of happy clucking noises happening.

'Chickens are very sociable animals,' Auntie Rita signed. 'They're not supposed to live alone. They get sad without companionship.'

'Like people,' Carla said, and Lizzie nodded.

'These four chickens have been through so much together,' Lizzie signed. She gave Rosie a stroke when she came over to her. Rosie felt warm and soft.

'Will Rosie's feathers grow back?' Ted wanted to know.

Auntie Rita smiled and signed: 'All of the chickens I've rescued over the years – and there have been lots – even the ones with very few feathers, have all grown their feathers back. It's amazing what a good diet and lots of tender loving care can do. But first we need to take this cloak off Rosie. It might have seemed like a good way to keep her nice and warm, but the truth is that the wool will damage any tiny new feathers trying to grow, and I think this would be especially so with the soft feathers of a Silkie chicken.'

Mum, Dad and Ona came to see Rosie with her friends.

'We thought she was a tiny dinosaur at first,' Ted signed. 'Did you know chickens are even more closely related to the T-rex than crocodiles are? I learnt it from one of my dinosaur books.'

Mum shook her head. 'That's amazing, Ted,' she signed.

'I'd never turn any animal in need away from the sanctuary. Not even if

Rosie had been a real dinosaur!' Auntie Rita signed, and everyone laughed.

Lizzie smiled. She was very glad Rosie had been reunited with her friends, and **the mystery of the lost chicken had been solved**.

CHAPTER 14

Once they'd settled Rosie and finished preparing the greenhouse, Lizzie took Lucky back to the house so she could have a snooze. Auntie Rita video-called her volunteers to help spread the word about the chicks, and the volunteers called other animal helpers.

A chicken rescue organization offered to take a number of them. Other people brought heat lamps to the sanctuary, as well as their expert knowledge.

'For the first few weeks after chicks are born, they can't regulate their own body temperature,' Auntie Rita explained to Lizzie and Ted. 'That's what mum chickens are for. Baby chicks tuck themselves under their mum's feathers – all nice and warm – but these chicks don't have mums, so they need **heat lamps**!

Everyone wanted to help, and in no time at all the chicks' story went viral. The local TV news did a piece on the plight of the homeless chicks and even interviewed Chester in his hospital bed.

'The sale of Baron's farmland to Butterbrooks will no longer go ahead. But that leaves many tiny chicks looking for new homes,' the newsreader said.

The piece was picked up by the national – and then the international – news too.

★

Ted heard the lorry's horn blast, but Lizzie had already seen it through the window. The chicks were here!

In the back of the lorry was crate stacked upon crate of tiny yellow birds. The stacks were almost as tall as Lizzie's dad when they were unloaded.

Lizzie could see the tiny chicks inside them, but they weren't going to let them out until they were safely in the big greenhouse.

Carla, O.B. and Ona arrived with the sacks of special chick food. There was water already in the greenhouse for them.

'They're called one-day-old chicks, although they can be up to seventy-two hours old,' Auntie Rita signed, as they released the little yellow babies into the greenhouse. 'They don't even get to meet their mums as they're hatched in an incubator before being sent out to farms. It's such a shame, because chicken mums love their chicks and will do anything to protect them. They even cluck to them when they're still in their eggs, so even before a chick is hatched it's able to recognize its mother by the sound of her voice.'

'We watched some chicks hatching in an incubator at school,' Ted signed. 'They were so cute, like little balls of fluff. But no one was allowed to take them home. I think they got sent back to the farm.' Now he looked worried. 'And then I don't know what happened to them.'

Auntie Rita squeezed his arm. 'The main thing is that you're helping lots and lots of chickens now,' she signed. Then she gave Lizzie and Ted a chick each to hold. 'Be very careful – they're fragile and can be very wriggly.'

Lizzie and Ted were very gentle and held the chicks in both hands. They were **so so soft**. Then Ted gave his chick back to Rita and went to phone his gran.

Auntie Rita smiled at Lizzie before signing, 'These chickens are going to have a proper life, thanks to you. A kind life.'

CHAPTER 15

Very early the next morning, Lizzie looked out of the caravan window to see car after car driving up to the sanctuary. People were arriving to take the chicks home.

The news about them had spread throughout the world.

'My sister in New Zealand saw the chicks on TV and texted me about them,' one lady told Lizzie, who lipread her.

'My grandkids are in California. They told us we simply had to adopt some of

the chicks, and so here we are,' Lizzie saw someone tell O.B..

One man was shaking Auntie Rita's hand. 'Thank you for all the wonderful work you do and all the animals you've rescued,' he said. Lizzie saw Auntie Rita quickly brush away a tear as she lipread him.

A lot of the chicks had already gone with the chicken rescue people during the night. Now it was time for the rest of them to become pets. Auntie Rita, her volunteers, plus the chicken specialists, had been up all night, and the chicks were ready and waiting to go.

Lizzie smiled as person after person came forward with their boxes lined with straw to take their new pets home.

Auntie Rita and her volunteers scattered some feed in each of the boxes before putting the chicks inside them. They didn't want the little birds to get hungry on their journey. The chicks left in pairs, so they wouldn't get lonely either.

'It's finally time for us to go home too,' Mum signed, as they waved the last car off.

Lizzie clipped Lucky's car harness on.

'Please don't go just yet,' a voice called out to them. It was Chester Baron and he was with his part-time assistant, Jennifer.

Lucky didn't bark at Chester this time. She wagged her tail instead. Lizzie noticed Chester was holding something.

'This should help with the bills for a

little while,' the old man said to Rita as Ted translated for him. It was a cheque. A cheque for a lot of money!

'Thank you, Chester,' Rita signed. 'Thank you so much.'

'No – thank you,' Chester said, and he turned to Lizzie and Lucky. 'I'll never forget you helping me,' he added. 'I could feel your hand holding mine, and I knew I would be OK.'

Lizzie made the sign for 'you're welcome'.

Chester smiled sadly and started to speak. 'All of my life I've been fascinated by dinosaurs. I should have been a palaeontologist, not a farmer – this area of the country is excellent for finding fossils, as you know. But the farm's been in my family since the 1800s, and I wanted to provide for my family.' Chester paused for a moment to clear his throat. 'My wife's gone now, and my daughter's not been in touch since she left. She's leading her own life somewhere. It's time for me to do the same. I see now it's important to be brave and follow what's in your heart.' He looked over at Ivan and the other palaeontologists wistfully. 'Though it's probably too late . . . '

Lizzie shook her head. She was sure Ivan and the other palaeontologists would welcome Chester's help on the dig. It looked like there might be a lot of fossils both at the sanctuary and on Chester's farm – fossils that had been hidden in the soft clay soil for millions of years.

'This is for you, to say thank you,' Chester said, pulling something small from his pocket and holding it out to

Lizzie. 'I thought you might like it.'

Lizzie took the smooth stone from him and frowned. She could see strange patterns inside it.

'What is it?' she signed.

'It's a stromatolite. A fossil containing some of the first signs of life on Earth. It's fossilized blue-green algae in limestone,' Chester told her through Ted.

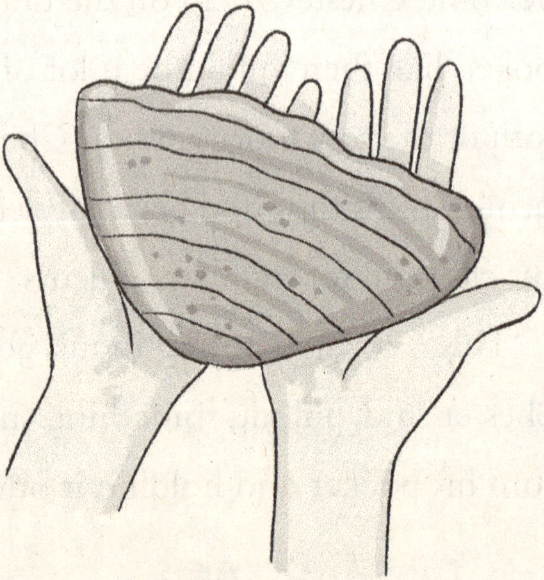

Lizzie's mouth fell open. It was an **amazing gift**.

'How old is it?' Ted asked Chester.

'Oh, at least a billion years,' Chester told him. 'Maybe three and a half billion.'

Lizzie clutched the fossil to her and thanked him. She would treasure it always.

★

Lizzie and her family had finished packing up.

'Time to go home,' signed Dad, as he turned the key in the car's ignition. Ted looked down at the small box he was holding on his lap and smiled. The two chicks inside it were chirping. His gran had said they could have some as long as he promised to build them a chicken coop so they could go outside when they were old enough. For now they were going to stay in his bedroom. He'd got a long list of instructions from Carla on how to keep his chicks happy and healthy.

'My gran said she kept chickens when she was my age,' Ted signed to Lizzie, and Lizzie smiled.

She was looking forward to seeing the little chicks grow up. They'd probably enjoy an adventure garden like Ted's rabbits, and also some toys.

Lucky picked up her octopus toy and Lizzie gave her a stroke. Then Lucky climbed on to Lizzie's lap, and Lizzie and Ted waved and waved through the back window as they drove off.

Auntie Rita, Kendo and Asta, Gloria, Elmo and Sweet, Marigold and Moon, Lulu, Herbert, Peggy and Priscilla were at the gates to see them off. Rosie was sitting on Carla's shoulder, and Ona and O.B. had Tesha, Grace and Bunty under their arms. Chester and Jennifer were with them too, and Ivan, Margaret and the teams of palaeontologist and archaeologists came to join them.

Lizzie saw Chester talking to Ivan and smiled. He was just as excited about finding fossils as she was at finding clues and solving mysteries.

CHAPTER 16

A few months later, Lizzie, Lucky, Ted and Lizzie's mum and dad went back to the Five Freedoms Animal Sanctuary for the weekend.

Auntie Rita was waiting for them at the gate along with Herbert, Lulu and Peggy. The sanctuary looked quite different and had even more animals than it had done before, as the cows and sheep from Chester's farm were living there now too.

'I might need you to help me with some more painting. . .' Auntie Rita told Lizzie's mum and dad, and they signed back that they were happy to help.

Lizzie pointed to the three orphan kittens – the ones who'd crawled over Lucky lying on the mat in the summer. They were with an older cat now. Auntie Rita nodded and signed that the kittens' mother had arrived the morning after they'd left. They weren't orphans any more.

'They were so happy to see her and she was so happy to see them. She licked and licked them,' Auntie Rita signed.

The poorly sheep and her lamb who'd been staying in Auntie Rita's house were now both well too, and out in the paddock. The lamb ran around and kicked his heels with the goats, Elmo and Sweet, while the mother sheep and Gloria chewed on some hay.

'We've got so much more space now Chester's given us half of his farmland too,' Auntie Rita signed. 'Of course, at the moment the archaeologists are doing more investigations there, and Chester's happy for them to do so. He gets so excited every time they find something.'

‘What’s he doing with the other half of his farm?’ Mum asked.

‘He’s keeping that and growing crops on it for the sanctuary animals. He’s going to plant an orchard in the spring so Herbert can have even more apples,’ Auntie Rita signed, and Herbert whinnied as if he knew exactly what she meant.

‘Where is Chester?’ Lizzie asked, and Auntie Rita pointed to an old man wearing a white panama hat in the distance where the palaeontologists were digging. Carla was talking to him – she had Rosie with her. The chicken was sitting on her shoulder like a parrot and looked quite at home there. As Lizzie walked over to them, accompanied by Ted, she saw that Rosie's blue and lavender Silkie feathers had grown back, just as Auntie Rita had said they would. She looked so fluffy.

'Find anything interesting this morning?' Lizzie signed when she reached them.

Carla told her she'd been teaching Chester some sign language.

Chester chuckled and said, 'We've found lots of . . .' and then he carefully fingerspelt the letters: '**c–o–p–r–o–l–i–t–e**.'

'Ooh,' said Lizzie. 'What's that?'

Chester picked up a small piece of coprolite and showed it to her.

ANIMAL
RESCUE

'Have a guess?' Chester asked Lizzie, and Ted translated.

Lizzie shook her head, but Ted knew the answer.

'It's fossilized dinosaur **poo**!' he signed.

Lizzie looked at them both in amazement, but Ted was already laughing, and Chester laughed and laughed too.

Ted signed to Lizzie that Chester's laugh sounded like it had been living inside the old man for a long time, just waiting to burst out. And then Lizzie started laughing too.

'In the second half of the 1800s, lots and lots of coprolite was found in this area. It was used as fertilizer for crops,' Chester told them. 'They even used it on the Baron family farm back then.'

Lucky, who'd been watching them all, suddenly started digging in the clay soil. Ivan ran over to them as Lucky picked up something that looked a bit like a small ball in her jaws.

'That's not coprolite . . .' Ivan said, taking it carefully from Lucky. Lizzie lipread him. 'This looks like a fossilized wonderchicken's egg.'

'A wonderchicken?' said Ted.

'Its proper name is *Asteriornis*,' Ivan told him. 'They're the ancestors of modern-day chickens and ducks.'

'When did wonderchickens live?' Lizzie signed and Ted translated.

'Oh, roughly sixty-six million years

ago,' Ivan told her. 'Bird fossils from that time are extremely rare. It would have been alive when big dinosaurs like T-rex and triceratops were roaming the world.'

Lizzie and Ted looked at each other in amazement, as Lucky started digging again. Lizzie borrowed Margaret's archaeological trowel to try and help her. Lucky didn't just find one egg. Below it there was a complete, fossilized nest of eggs.

'This is incredible,' said Ivan.

'I told you, clay soil is perfect for finding fossils,' Chester said proudly, as everyone got back to work. 'I should have started doing this years ago.'

'At least you're doing it now,' Carla told him.

'Agreed,' Chester told her. 'This is the most fun I've ever had.'

A lady who looked a lot like Chester was walking towards them.

'Dad?' the lady called out, and Lizzie lipread. 'Dad!'

The effect on Mr Baron was instant.

'Emilia!' he cried, as he hurried to her as quickly as he could whilst leaning on his walking stick for support. The next moment, the two of them were hugging and laughing and hugging some more.

'A girl called Nora and her father contacted me in Australia. She showed me the news about what was happening to the farm, and I knew I had to come home and see you. I'm so happy and proud that you didn't sell the land,' Emilia said, and Ted translated.

'Me too,' Chester said, 'Me too.' His smile was so big it seemed to stretch right across his face.

Lizzie smiled as she took a photograph of father and daughter to send to Nora along with the message:

Excellent detective work ☺

*

'They found a huge dinosaur fossil in western Queensland recently,' Ted told Emilia later that day. 'It's called a plesiosaur and is about one hundred million years old. It lived in the sea and was a marine dinosaur.'

'I'd like to see that,' Chester said, and Emilia smiled.

'You should come to Australia and see it, Dad,' said Emilia. 'There's lots of dinosaur fossils in Australia.'

'Maybe I will,' Chester said with a smile. 'If they can spare me here.'

Mum, Dad and Auntie Rita came over with drinks and cake for everyone. Rosie

had her own pot of popcorn that she shared with Lucky.

'Rosie likes perching on my shoulder,' Carla told Lizzie and Ted. 'But if she needs a rest she goes in here.' Carla pressed the button of Lightning's secret compartment. Inside it they could see a soft comfy pillow for Rosie to rest on – as well as a few tasty treats. 'Once she's in there it's like

she's vanished. Although she can look out if she wants. One time I even heard her snoring.'

'Does Rosie live with you now?' Lizzie signed, as Lucky rolled over so Lizzie could give her full tummy a rub.

Carla laughed and shook her head. 'Rosie lives where she likes. Sometimes she spends time with me if I'm here – but mostly she likes to be with Tesha, Grace and Bunty.'

'So, did the chicken or the egg come first?' Dad signed to Chester, pointing at Rosie and then the wonderchicken eggs that Lucky had found.

The old man chuckled and squeezed his daughter's hand. 'Now that's a true mystery,' he said and Lizzie smiled, because she really loved mysteries.

THE END

THANK YOU

I met many amazing people and animals while writing this book and it has many elements in it that are very close to my heart. Writing this story made me both laugh and cry. I'm so happy to be able to share it with you.

The Deaf community throughout the world is welcoming and generous. I'm very grateful to all the friends I have in it for their love and support. I was happy and proud when the Royal Association of the Deaf agreed to translate *Lizzie and*

Lucky: The Mystery of the Missing Puppies, the first book in this series, into BSL with me signing the introduction.

Inspiration to write *The Mystery of the Lost Chicken* came from the animals and staff of the many rescue centres and sanctuaries I've visited. These are people who have devoted their whole lives to helping animals.

My husband, Eric, shares my love of animals and helped a lot with the research, as always. We both agree it's impossible not to smile when watching baby goats play with joyful abandon.

I feel so fortunate to be working with such a fantastic team at Puffin. My new editor, Katie Sinfield, has been a delight to work with and shared my vision, helping to steer Lizzie and Lucky on to their next adventure – thank you, Katie. Also, thank you to the wonderful copy-editor and fellow sign-language user, Pippa Shaw, plus my brilliant and insightful new copy-editor, Isabella Haigh. Thanks to Tim Budgen for vividly bringing the characters to life, along with designers Arabella Jones and Janene Spencer. Thanks also to publicist Lily Orgill, marketer Michelle Nathan, and the brilliant sales team of Rozzie Todd, Toni Budden and Kat Baker. Never forgetting my friend, and agent of twenty years, Clare Pearson. Thank you.

My golden retrievers, Freya and Ellie, are the best of office companions. They inspire me every day on our long walks by the river – and I'm overjoyed that we now have a family of otters living there!

Finally thank you to you – the reader for whom this story was written. I hope you enjoy it and feel inspired to write your own stories.

Megan

HOW TO KEEP YOUR PET CHICKEN HAPPY

Want to know how to properly care for your chicken friends? Here are some suggestions:

1. Make sure their home is clean and spacious

Chickens need a safe and comfortable place to eat, sleep and lay their eggs. They don't like being cooped up, so make sure their home is big enough to move around freely.

2. Feed them well

Just like humans, chickens need a balanced diet that includes fruit, vegetables and water.

3. Dust baths!

Chickens love a dust bath to keep any creepy-crawlies from getting under their feathers. Make sure your fluffy friends have a tray of dirt or dust that they can clean themselves in.

4. Give them space to play outside!

Chickens love to roam around somewhere they can play with their friends and peck around in the grass. Make sure they get time outside every day. They also love to play with toys and are very inquisitive. Some chickens like doing agility courses; others just like cuddles. They're all different, just like we are.

5. Give them lots of light

Daylight keeps your chickens happy and healthy. It also helps to regulate something called their *circadian rhythm,* which supports everything from how often they lay eggs to getting a good night's sleep!

6. Keep them safe

Foxes and bigger birds are always on the look-out to try and kidnap a chicken, so make sure their area is secure and protected.

7. Read to them

Chickens are social animals and love human interaction. Why not show your chickens some love and read your favourite story to them, or, if you're feeling creative, make one up as you go!

LEARN TO SIGN

Can you read the dedication at the front of the book using sign language?

A

B

C

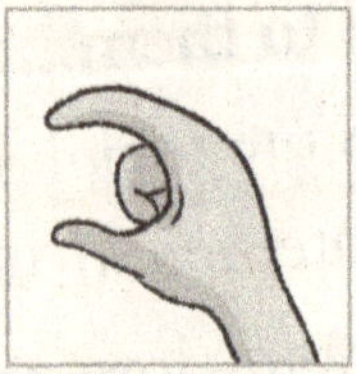

D

E

F

G

H

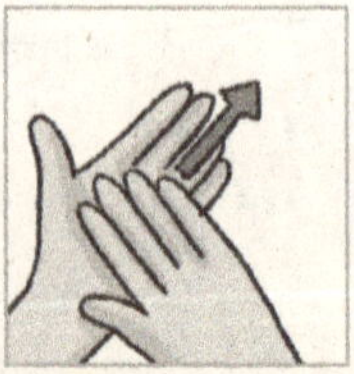

I

J

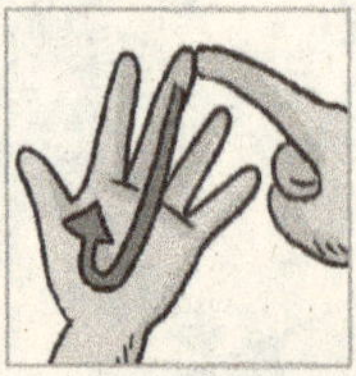

K

L

M

N

O

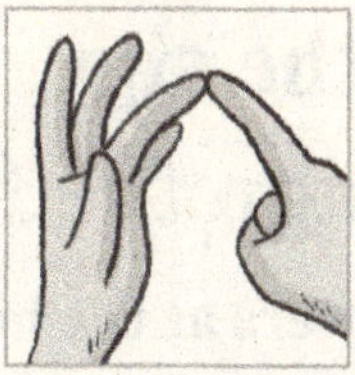

P

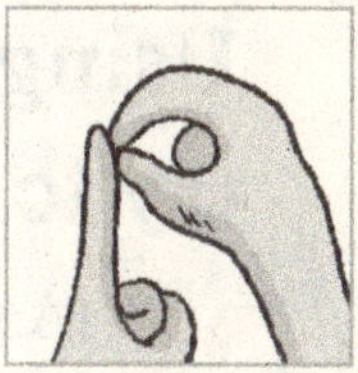

Q

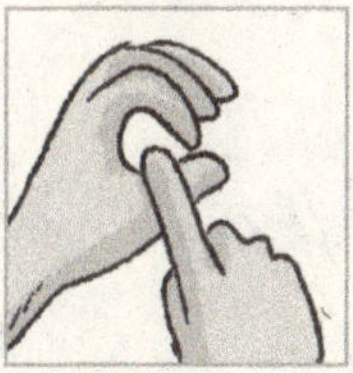

R

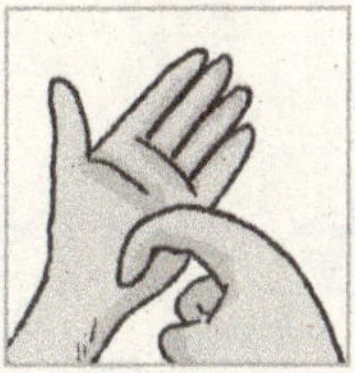

S

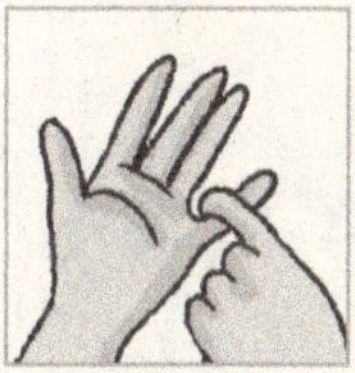

T

U

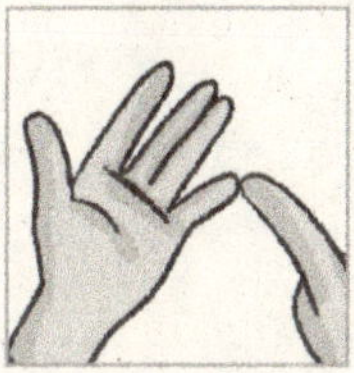

V

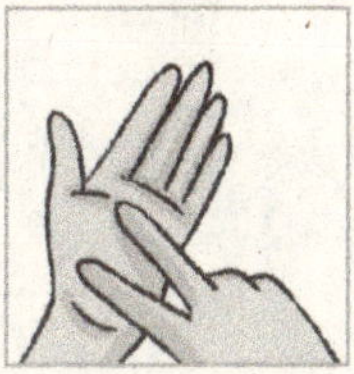

W

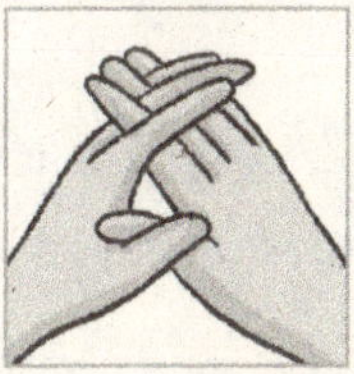

X

Y

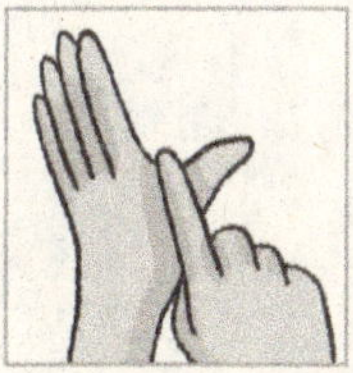

Z

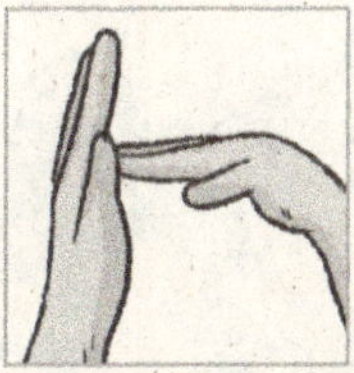

Using the sign-language guide, try to sign the following words:

(Answers at the bottom of the page.)

1 

2 

3 

4

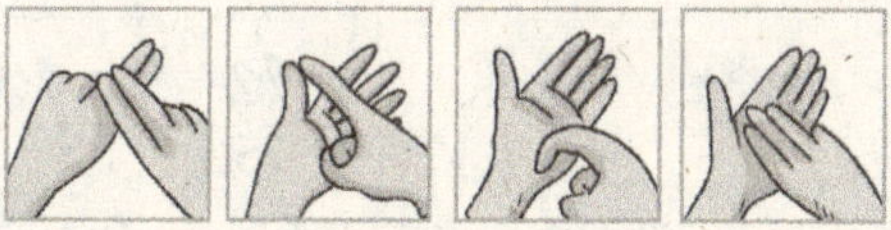

___ ___ ___ ___

5

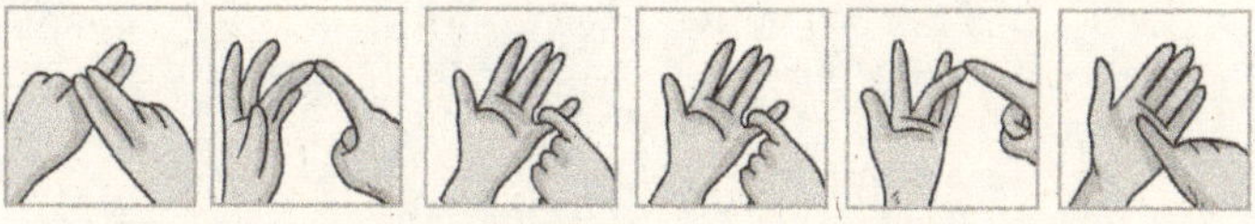

___ ___ ___ ___ ___ ___

6

___ ___ ___ ___ ___ ___ ___

Answers: 1: chicken, 2: otter,
3: sheep, 4: farm, 5: fossil, 6: kittens.

7

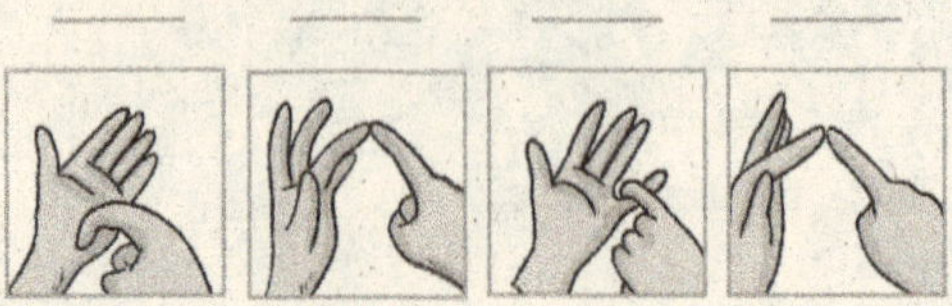

8

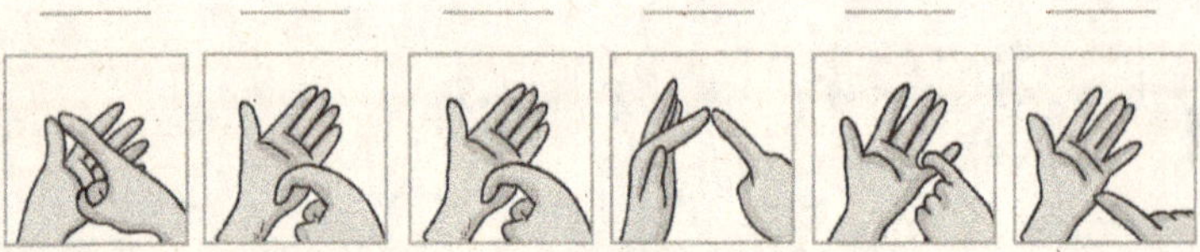

Answers: 7: rose, 8: arrest.

HOW TO BE A DETECTIVE

Feeling inspired by Lizzie and Lucky, and want to be a detective yourself?

First, you need the equipment.

This is what's inside Lizzie's detective bag:

- Binoculars
- Phone
- Magnifying glass
- White-and-black torch
- Torch
- Fingerprint kit
- Wildlife crime information leaflet
- Clue bag
- Tweezers
- Pack of tissues
- Detective gloves
- Lucky's dog whistle and ball
- Notebook and pencil

Next, you need to dress the part. Wear clothes that help you blend in – plain clothes would work well!

Then, in your notebook, begin writing things you notice about your surroundings. Every detective has a keen eye – that means they observe everything around them. Maybe look outside your window and note down everything you see.

You can use your torch to read invisible ink or inspect dark areas, perhaps under the sofa or your bed – you never know what you might find! If you see anything suspicious, use your tweezers to carefully pick it up and put it inside your clue bag.

You could even go outside to investigate further. Are there any footprints on the floor? Any trails of mud? Does anything look different to normal? Use your magnifying glass to really inspect the things around you. Note down your findings.

Once you've done this, you're well on your way to becoming a detective – your next step is to piece together your clues and find a mystery to solve . . .

Loved this book?
Check out
Lizzie and Lucky's
other adventures!

LiZZiE & LUCKY
The fabulous detective duo!
The Mystery of the Missing Puppies
ANIMAL RESCUE
Illustrated by Tim Budgen
Megan Rix

LIZZIE & LUCKY
The fabulous detective duo!
The Mystery of the Stolen Treasure
ANIMAL RESCUE
Illustrated by Tim Budgen
Megan Rix

Lizzie & Lucky
The fabulous detective duo!
The Mystery of the Disappearing Rabbit
Illustrated by Tim Budgen
Megan Rix